Ashes to Ink

Also from Carrie Ann Ryan

Montgomery Ink: Colorado Springs
Book 1: *Fallen Ink*
Book 2: *Restless Ink*
Book 2.5: Ashes to Ink
Book 3: *Jagged Ink*
Book 3.5: *Ink by Numbers*

The Fractured Connections Series:
A Montgomery Ink Spin Off Series
Book 1: *Breaking Without You*
Book 2: *Shouldn't Have You*
Book 3: *Falling With You*

The Montgomery Ink: Boulder Series:
Book 1: *Wrapped in Ink*

The Less Than Series:
A Montgomery Ink Spin Off Series
Book 1: *Breathless With Her*
Book 2: *Reckless With You*

The Elements of Five Series:
A YA Fantasy Series
Book 1: *From Breath and Ruin*

Montgomery Ink
Book 0.5: *Ink Inspired*
Book 0.6: *Ink Reunited*
Book 1: *Delicate Ink*
Book 1.5: *Forever Ink*
Book 2: *Tempting Boundaries*
Book 4: *Harder than Words*
Book 4: *Written in Ink*
Book 4.5: *Hidden Ink*
Book 5: *Ink Enduring*
Book 6: *Ink Exposed*

Book 4: *Enforcer's Redemption*
Book 4.5: *Blurred Expectations*
Book 4.7: *Forgiveness*
Book 5: *Shattered Emotions*
Book 6: *Hidden Destiny*
Book 6.5: *A Beta's Haven*
Book 7: *Fighting Fate*
Book 7.5: *Loving the Omega*
Book 7.7: *The Hunted Heart*
Book 8: *Wicked Wolf*
The Complete Redwood Pack Box Set (Contains Books 1-7.7)

Branded Packs (Written with Alexandra Ivy)
Book 1: *Stolen and Forgiven*
Book 2: *Abandoned and Unseen*
Book 3: *Buried and Shadowed*

Dante's Circle Series
Book 1: *Dust of My Wings*
Book 2: *Her Warriors' Three Wishes*
Book 3: *An Unlucky Moon*
The Dante's Circle Box Set (Contains Books 1-3)
Book 3.5: *His Choice*
Book 4: *Tangled Innocence*
Book 5: *Fierce Enchantment*
Book 6: *An Immortal's Song*
Book 7: *Prowled Darkness*
The Complete Dante's Circle Series (Contains Books 1-7)

Holiday, Montana Series
Book 1: *Charmed Spirits*
Book 2: *Santa's Executive*
Book 3: *Finding Abigail*
The Holiday Montana Box Set (Contains Books 1-3)
Book 4: *Her Lucky Love*
Book 5: *Dreams of Ivory*
The Complete Holiday, Montana Box Set (Contains Books 1-5)

Ashes to Ink

A Montgomery Ink:
Colorado Springs Novella

By Carrie Ann Ryan

1001 Dark Nights

EVIL EYE
CONCEPTS

Ashes to Ink
A Montgomery Ink: Colorado Springs Novella
By Carrie Ann Ryan

1001 Dark Nights

Copyright 2019 Carrie Ann Ryan
ISBN: 978-1-948050-85-2

Foreword: Copyright 2014 M. J. Rose

Published by Evil Eye Concepts, Incorporated

Acknowledgments from the Author

Being with 1001 Dark Nights is always an honor. I wasn't ready to write this story, had never planned on Ryan or Abby getting books of their own. Then, after Abby's tragedy, readers wanted her to have an HEA.

I wasn't ready.

Then Liz asked me what characters I wanted to write this year and there were only two in my heart, despite not being ready emotionally.

So yes, thanks to Liz, MJ, Jillian, and Chelle, Abby and Ryan get their HEA…even if I felt like I wasn't ready. But those two deserved their HEA, no matter where my heart was during that time.

So thank you ladies. Thank you for everything.

Sign up for the 1001 Dark Nights Newsletter
and be entered to win a Tiffany Key necklace.

There's a contest every month!

Go to www.1001DarkNights.com to subscribe.

As a bonus, all subscribers can download
FIVE FREE exclusive books!

One Thousand and One Dark Nights

Once upon a time, in the future...

*I was a student fascinated with stories and learning.
I studied philosophy, poetry, history, the occult, and
the art and science of love and magic. I had a vast
library at my father's home and collected thousands
of volumes of fantastic tales.*

*I learned all about ancient races and bygone
times. About myths and legends and dreams of all
people through the millennium. And the more I read
the stronger my imagination grew until I discovered
that I was able to travel into the stories... to actually
become part of them.*

*I wish I could say that I listened to my teacher
and respected my gift, as I ought to have. If I had, I
would not be telling you this tale now.
But I was foolhardy and confused, showing off
with bravery.*

*One afternoon, curious about the myth of the
Arabian Nights, I traveled back to ancient Persia to
see for myself if it was true that every day Shahryar
(Persian: شهریار, "king") married a new virgin, and then
sent yesterday's wife to be beheaded. It was written
and I had read, that by the time he met Scheherazade,
the vizier's daughter, he'd killed one thousand
women.*

Something went wrong with my efforts. I arrived in the midst of the story and somehow exchanged places with Scheherazade — a phenomena that had never occurred before and that still to this day, I cannot explain.

Now I am trapped in that ancient past. I have taken on Scheherazade's life and the only way I can protect myself and stay alive is to do what she did to protect herself and stay alive.

Every night the King calls for me and listens as I spin tales. And when the evening ends and dawn breaks, I stop at a point that leaves him breathless and yearning for more. And so the King spares my life for one more day, so that he might hear the rest of my dark tale.

As soon as I finish a story... I begin a new one... like the one that you, dear reader, have before you now.

Chapter One

Abby loved tea. She loved everything about it. The taste, the smell, the way it warmed her up on a cold day or cooled her down on a warm one. She'd even loved tea when she was a little girl, playing with air in her teacups and treating her stuffed animals and Cabbage Patch dolls to an afternoon tea party.

Her grandmother had taught her the basics of brewing the perfect cuppa, as well as the ratio of sugar cubes needed. Abby had then learned to try tea with all additives: cinnamon sticks, lemon wedges, a dash of cream. Some might consider that ruining it, but Abby had wanted to try it all.

She loved tea bags but adored loose-leaf tea even more. She relished steeping it, blending it, and finding the perfect mix for the season.

So when she found herself looking for a way to create something that was just *hers* and start over after everything had fallen apart around her, opening the tea shop had seemed like a no-brainer.

Teas'd specialized in loose-leaf tea, but Abby also sold some bagged tea and different teapots and helpful equipment.

It was Abby's goal in life to make it so others could discover the joys of tea like she had, and maybe find a new favorite along the way. She had always loved the idea of teatime, even if she didn't have the time to truly sit down and enjoy it herself every day.

Regardless, she adored the scents, loved the idea of falling into a cup—a different flavor every day. With the resurgence of tea drinkers, it was easier for Abby to find fellow tea lovers as time moved on. There were big chain tea shops and smaller ones as well, but Teas'd was just for her. She was a tiny little speck in the idea of tea and how it could serve the needs of the people, but she was the best speck she could possibly be.

She'd had to be after everything changed.

She'd had to be when she lost everything.

Well, not everything. She still had her little girl. Abby grinned down at her phone and swiped up so she could look at the photo on the home screen.

Julia was growing every day and even looked slightly different now than she had in the picture. Abby still couldn't quite believe that she and Max had made this beautiful baby girl. Max might not be around to help raise Julia, but he had been there for the conception and had been there to pick out everything the two of them as new parents would need to raise their child together.

It didn't hurt as much as it once had to think about Max. Oh, it would always hurt, but at least it didn't make Abby want to throw up and grieve right then.

She could think about her husband and smile now. She could think about the fact that he had loved her with all of his heart, even if that had been the thing to take him away from her in the end.

And she couldn't say her feelings didn't matter now though, because that would be a disgrace to his memory and the fact that she could see Max in her little girl every single day.

Julia would never know her father, but Abby was doing her best to make sure that Julia knew exactly who Max was, and how excited he had been to have Julia in his life.

The two had never met, but Abby knew Max was always watching over them.

There was no other way to think about it. Not when Abby needed to get up every day and breathe—try to be the mom and woman she needed to be.

But today was a new day, just like all the others. Today, she would make some tea, sell some tea, and maybe even have a cookie or two. Because it was Friday, and she was allowed to have a cookie if she wanted.

She just might have a little extra padding on her hips, but that was fine with her. It wasn't like she was trying to entice a man.

Oh, she'd dated a couple of times in the past year or so, but it hadn't really amounted to much. She hadn't been ready, and she didn't know if she was ready now either.

"What are you looking at over there?"

Abby looked up at the sound of her friend Adrienne's voice and smiled. Adrienne Montgomery owned the tattoo shop, Montgomery Ink Too, next door and was part of a huge family—way bigger than just the set of cousins that lived near Abby.

The Montgomerys were large, loud, brash, and the sweetest people Abby had ever known. They had taken her in with just one look, much like their cousins in Denver had, and Abby loved every single one of them.

"Just looking at tea," Abby answered, holding up a couple of tins. "I'm trying to see what I need to put on special. We have good stock of most things, but not all."

"I don't know how you do it. I mean, I know how to run a business, and I think I'm doing pretty well, but it takes the advice of two accountants for me to know what I'm doing."

"Since I have the same two accountants you do, I totally understand."

Shea was Adrienne's sister-in-law, and Roxie was Adrienne's sister. Both were accountants, and pretty much helped run the businesses on this stretch.

The Montgomerys owned two of the businesses—Montgomery Ink Too, and Colorado Icing. While Adrienne and Shep ran the tattoo shop, the Montgomerys' middle sister, Thea, owned the bakery at the end of the strip.

Abby had a feeling that if there had been more space available, the accountants of the family probably would have moved in as well. Or maybe even the mechanic, Carter, who was married to Roxie. In fact, Adrienne was dating one of the tattoo artists, Mace, and that just meant there was more family than ever. More Montgomerys.

Abby didn't think that Thea's boyfriend, Dimitri, would be able to move a whole high school into the strip, but if there were a way, the Montgomerys would likely make it happen.

"Your family really is pretty amazing." Abby grinned as Adrienne rolled her eyes.

"Oh, don't tell the guys that. I mean, you can tell me, Thea, and Roxie. It's true, and it's sort of what we do. We are the touchstone for the Montgomerys."

They both laughed at that because even though it might be true, every single one of the Montgomerys had their own touchstones when it came to what those around them needed.

"So, have any good tea for me today?" Adrienne asked. "I have a long project coming up, one that's gonna take me a few hours and a few sessions. I could use all the energy I can get. And while I love coffee from Thea's bakery, I think I'm in the mood for tea today. Something to keep me wired, but something flavorful as well. I can head over to Thea's later for something sugary, or even a sandwich for some protein, but here is where I want my tea."

"Well, you've come to the right place. Let me set you up with some chai. I know that's your favorite." Abby went around the counter and began working. She knew the exact blend her friend favored and even had the milk Adrienne so dearly loved to put in it. She'd make a latte if she could, but she only did that when she visited Thea's bakery. Here at Teas'd, it was all about the blends and steeping.

"That and some of that peppermint one for later. It is the holidays. You have some peppermint, too, right?" Adrienne bounced from foot to foot as if she'd already had her caffeine for the day. Knowing Adrienne, she probably had but wanted more. Abby was happy to oblige.

"Oh, I have the peppermint. I also have that white chocolate peppermint bark one that you love." Both of them smiled, and Abby watched as Adrienne rubbed her stomach with her hand, her eyes comically wide.

"I might have to come back for that later."

"I can always stop by with some tea. That is what I'm here for."

"You're going to be a delivery person for tea as well?"

"I can. Only for my friends."

Abby didn't actually serve brewed tea all that often. Most people came to Teas'd for stock rather than just a cuppa. But she did have a couple of places to sit outside, as well as one inside. It was winter in Colorado Springs, so sitting outside wasn't something that people did often.

But Abby knew some *did* like to sit outside the bakery at the other end of the strip, drinking their hot cocoa or coffee and braving the cold just because they were Coloradans, and that's what they did.

And while it didn't happen often, she loved when people came in for a cup to go, or even stayed to drink out of her ceramic mugs. She had painstakingly searched forever for the cups that she wanted and had ended up just going to Jake Gallagher to have them made.

Jake was an artist. He sculpted with his hands and with his heart. He'd made the mugs for her, as well as other things she could sell in the store.

She knew that he made art. *Real* art. And though she thought of her teashop as its own kind of art—the way it made others feel was art itself—she knew Jake was in a realm of his own.

With any other person, he might not have tried to help her as he did, but they had a good relationship now, and she liked that their working relationship meant that she could sell his wares and still use everything that he made for her and her customers.

The Gallaghers were connected to the Montgomerys through marriage, and Abby was tied to the Gallaghers through Max since Jake's brother Murphy had been one of Max's best friends.

It was odd how everything seemed to tie together and be so close—yet so far away.

She might have felt that she was on the outside looking in once, but that wasn't the case anymore. The Montgomerys and the Gallaghers wouldn't allow that.

And while both families had given her space to breathe, they hadn't given her enough room to bury herself. No, she wasn't thinking physically, she would never do that. Never to herself, never to Julia, and never to Max's memory.

But she had needed some time to figure out how to be a single mom in this world. A mom without a real job and with only a savings account for a dream that she'd never thought to have realized in the timeframe she was forced to work in.

"That smells delicious," Adrienne said. "Seriously delicious."

Abby smiled, knowing today would be a good day, because it had to be. There was no other option when it came to tea.

"Here's the chai, just for you. I put it in a to-go cup, but if you want it out of a mug later, just let me know. I don't know how you and your elbows are doing today."

Adrienne rolled her eyes. "That was Ryan's fault, not mine. He startled me, and my elbow broke that mug. I paid for it. I went right up to Denver to ask Jake for another one. I am still so sorry about that."

Abby just smiled and shook her head, handing over the tea. "I know it wasn't your fault. I was just teasing. Though I do have to watch out for all of you over at the shop. You are a wild bunch."

Adrienne threw her head back and laughed. "That we are. Although, I do have to say, Ryan might be the wildest of us all." Adrienne winked.

Abby frowned at that but didn't say anything. Was Adrienne trying to match up two of her single friends? She wasn't sure if she was ready for anything like that. Or if she could think about Ryan like that at all.

He was handsome, that was for sure. And he always had a soft smile for Abby and was really great with Julia whenever they ran into each other. But that wasn't often since Julia was usually with the sitter when Abby was working. Or maybe Abby was just reading into what Adrienne had said because she'd had a little too much caffeine that morning. It was time to switch to herbal tea for the rest of the day if this was how she was going to start thinking.

"You better hurry if you're going to make your appointment. I'll be over later with any tea you need. Just call if you want something different than the peppermint. Or if Mace or any of the others need anything."

Adrienne leaned over and hugged Abby hard before taking her chai. "That I can do. It's just me, Mace, and Ryan over there. It's Shep's day off to hang out with the kiddos."

"I'm glad that you guys are able to work it out with all the kids. Daisy is with Shep as well?"

"Yes. Since we're able to make our schedules work, we don't have to get an outside sitter as much." Adrienne paused. "You know, Julia's always welcome to come over. I know that you would trade off with us if you could. You don't have to pay for a sitter. We Montgomerys make it work, and you *are* an honorary Montgomery, after all." Abby didn't shake her head or say no. She knew the others were just trying to help, but it was sometimes hard to willingly accept help when she wanted to stand on her own two feet. Plus, Abby didn't want to have to rely on anyone. Everything could change in an instant.

She shook off that thought and tried not to think about what it meant. She knew she was thinking about Max and the fact that she hadn't really spoken to his family since the funeral. They hadn't even met their granddaughter. Hadn't been involved in anything having to do with Julia's life. But that was okay. Abby would be okay. She had to be okay.

"I will talk to you later. And bring the tea." Adrienne just rolled her eyes. Probably because Abby hadn't commented about the daycare, but it didn't matter.

The Montgomerys would just bring it up again, and Abby would cave—because she would. Julia loved hanging out with Daisy and Livvy. And since Julia and Livvy were close to the same age, it worked out well. Soon, there would probably be more babies in the Montgomery world. They might not have room for Julia.

Abby shook that thought out of her head as Adrienne walked out of the store. And then she went back to work. There were more teas to make, more blends to perfect. And peppermint tea and chocolate to give to her friends later.

The day went on like normal. People came in for tea, and more than one for gift baskets and Christmas presents. The holidays were quickly approaching. So fast that Abby was sure she was behind on her shopping. She tried to get some things for the Montgomerys, but most everything was for Julia. She didn't want her daughter to assume there would always be gifts, something material. But she also wanted to spoil her baby just enough.

Julia deserved to be spoiled.

When Abby went to bring over peppermint tea for both Mace and Adrienne, Ryan was out on a personal call. She hadn't asked why, and she didn't want to explore why her brain immediately went to her wanting to know more about the man.

She shouldn't want to know more about him. He was a friend. Nothing more. And that meant she shouldn't be thinking about how he looked in his jeans every day. Or how much she liked the beautiful ink on his arms.

Nope, she wouldn't be thinking about any of that, thank you very much.

As the day wore on, the snow started to fall a little faster, a little harder. It had even begun to accumulate, which annoyed her since the forecast hadn't predicted it. Then again, the meteorologists were rarely right these days.

Abby wasn't really looking forward to driving in the snow, but she was a native Coloradan, and she was used to it. There was no use complaining about the precipitation in Colorado. That was like complaining that there were mountains or high altitude.

Weather like this was just something one got used to. The snow would probably melt the next day anyway. Even if the sun shone and it was frigid outside, the precipitation did its own thing here in Colorado.

As she made her way to the babysitter's house to pick up Julia, Abby knew that she would eventually have to ask the Montgomerys for help. She didn't like how long it took to get to the sitter's. If Julia stayed with one of the Montgomerys, she would actually be closer to Abby throughout the day, and Abby would have an easier and shorter drive home. It just made sense, and it would help out more people if she were there to add to the days when someone could watch all of the children.

She knew she just had to give up control and say yes.

But as the snow started to come down a little more earnestly, Abby was afraid she might have a bit of a hard time getting to her daughter tonight. And when she finally got there, it might be even more difficult to get them home. Her windshield wipers flew back and forth, the speed increasing, but so did the quickness of the snowfall.

She cursed herself once again for saying no to the Montgomerys.

When she finally arrived, Julia was hyper but not too much since Abby knew the babysitter didn't give her extra sugar. This was just Julia's happy, bubbly way. Her daughter was an amazing baby girl—though she wasn't really a baby anymore, was she?

Julia was perfect in every way. No, Abby wouldn't tell her that she was perfect over and over again because that would probably lead to issues down the road. But in Abby's mind, her daughter was perfect.

She had gone through so much in her short life, even before she was born.

She was a survivor. Just like Abby.

Her daughter spread joy to everyone, even if she was a little shy at times. But she was so graceful, so grateful. She shared her toys with others, and always had a smile for those who might not want to. If another kid was crying or just needed a hug, Julia was right there. Sometimes even faster than the adults in the room.

In the car, Julia babbled on about her day, using strings of words that wouldn't really make any sense to anyone but Abby. Because that was the role of the mother, to always understand what her baby girl was saying, even if it didn't make a lick of sense.

Darkness started to fall across Colorado. The fact that it was December meant that there weren't many hours of sunlight these days. The snow fell harder, the wind getting a little bit brisker. Abby just wanted to get home. She just wanted to *be* home.

She was just turning onto the next street in her route, knowing she was close to home but not close enough, when her tires slid on the ice that she hadn't seen.

She tried not to panic, tried to remember what she was supposed to do in this situation. She didn't twist her wheel hard, but she did try to turn into the skid. It was no use.

She was sliding into the other lane of traffic, and though there were no cars right now, that didn't mean there wouldn't be some soon. Julia didn't make a sound, Abby wasn't even sure she knew that something bad was happening.

Inside her head, Abby was screaming, her hands tight on the wheel—so tight, she was afraid she'd lose circulation.

But she couldn't focus on any of that. She just had to concentrate on making sure they survived the skid. She had to make sure that whatever they hit, they didn't hit too hard.

The sound of her tires sliding across the ice seemed loud in the vacuum of her panic.

It shouldn't have sounded loud. But the rubber did squeal, and Julia let out a sound in response that made Abby want to turn. But she couldn't. She had to keep her eyes on the road. The decision to do that, to not look at her baby girl when her daughter might need her, broke her. But she had to focus on what was in front of her.

The car hit the snowbank on the other side of the street with a dull thud, not even jostling the vehicle as it did, and Abby just sat there for a moment, her heartbeat so loud in her ears she couldn't hear anything else.

Everything had moved so slowly—and still did, as if she hadn't just been in a minor accident.

No other cars were coming, and there was no one else on the road. She always took this route because there was less traffic and fewer idiots out and about.

But it was cold, and there was nobody around to help. Her car was still running, but she was halfway in a ditch and slammed into a snowbank. Her body didn't hurt, but her head did. Only because of the headache, not anything else.

But Julia.

Oh my God. Julia.

Abby undid her seatbelt, trying to ignore the fact that she just might pass out from the stress, and tuning out the cheery Christmas music filling her car. This seemed like the worst time for Christmas music, but then again, she didn't know when a good time for it would be anymore.

When she finally got turned around, Julia just smiled and held out her hands for a hug. Abby practically crawled over the seat back to check on her baby girl. They hadn't hit hard, neither of them getting jarred too badly. The car hadn't even been going fast enough for the airbags to go off.

Abby knew that she needed to figure out how to get out of the ditch. Maybe she should call Carter. Or the cops. Then, she remembered that Roxie's husband Carter had just been in an accident and wasn't working at his shop. He wouldn't be operating the tow truck.

Right then, all Abby wanted to do was cry because she had no idea what to do.

But because she knew her baby was fine, that both of them were fine, she got Julia out of her car seat and held her close.

She had to keep reminding herself that they were okay. She wasn't even shaking, even though she probably should have been. Shock would likely do that to her later, but right now, she needed to hold her baby girl.

Headlights suddenly filled the car, and Abby closed her eyes and held Julia close, trying to protect her as best she could.

If a car hit them right then, Abby knew that they were done for.

But as the light continued to fill her car, the oncoming vehicle slowed.

The sound of a door opening and closing filled Abby's ears, followed by the sounds of a person walking, their shoes crunching on the snow.

Someone tapped on the window and called out her name.

Her name.

They knew her.

But because she and Julia had fogged up the windows, Abby couldn't see who it was. She scooted over in the backseat and opened the car door.

"Ryan," she breathed. "Ryan."

She had never been happier to see his bearded face.

Ryan frowned down at her, looked at Julia in her arms, and let out a soft curse. "Are you okay, Abby? What the hell happened?"

She just looked at him, and then promptly burst into tears.

Chapter Two

Ryan didn't know what to do with tears. Not a woman's tears, but tears in general. And when Abby started crying right in front of him, he was pretty sure he wanted to cry right along with her.

When he saw the car in front of him slide on that patch of ice, his blood had gone cold at the sight. Then, he'd noticed *who* was in that car, and he'd had to swallow down bile before he knocked on the window.

He'd known that Abby and Julia lived close to him, but the fact that they were close enough that he'd witnessed that? He wasn't sure if it was a blessing or a curse.

Ryan looked on as Julia patted her mother's cheek and murmured sweet nothings, clearly anxious that her mom was upset and not sure what to do about it.

So, Ryan did the only thing *he* could. He plucked Julia from Abby's arms and propped her up on his hip, grateful that she had her big, puffy jacket on to deal with the icy wind.

"You okay?" he asked again. "I mean physically, since Julia is out of her car seat and you're in the back."

Abby nodded, seeming to collect herself. He'd never seen her break before. She was always so cool and collected, even with those warm smiles of hers. It honestly scared him a little.

She wiped her tears and nodded. "We weren't going that fast but I hit the ice wrong."

"I can tell. Let's get that car seat into my vehicle. We'll make sure Julia is nice and warm, then deal with the technical aspects of this since I don't think I can pull your car out."

She sighed and nodded. "Thank you, Ryan. I didn't realize you were here. I mean…why are you here?"

He pointed at his house near the end of the street. "I live right there. Was on my way home from the shop and saw your car hit. I'm going to call Carter's place and get a tow truck out here. They'll deal with it and take photos for insurance and all that. I can take you home and make sure Julia gets warm. Sound like a deal?"

A little line formed between Abby's brows as she thought over his words. "Carter isn't at his shop."

Ryan gave her a tight nod. "I know." He kissed Julia's hand as she patted his face. She smiled at him, and he did the same to her, though he knew it probably didn't reach his eyes. Watching Abby and Julia crash like that hadn't made it easy to smile. Then remembering that Carter wasn't working because he'd almost died? Yeah, that made it harder to smile. "Carter's crew is working, though."

"Oh. I forgot." Abby was too damn pale.

"You're in your head. Take Julia and let me get the seat out of your car. I'll make a call. You two just stay and get warm." He paused. "You sure you're okay? Should we call an ambulance?"

She seemed to shake herself out of her thoughts and then stood up, her arms held out for her daughter. She once again looked like the woman he knew that could handle anything. The fact that she'd broken just a little in front of him told him not only how shaken she was, but also how damn strong she was to even allow herself to break down in the first place.

It took a hell of a person to show any kind of weakness in front of another, even though they weren't exactly strangers.

"Thank you, Ryan. I'm fine. Though I'll take Julia to her pediatrician tomorrow just in case. Neither of us hit our heads or anything, but I want to make sure she's okay."

"You're a good mom. Let's get you taken care of."

"Thank you, Ryan. For everything."

Ryan leaned down and ran his finger down Abby's cheek. From the look on her face, the action surprised them both. He quickly moved his hand, holding back a wince. He and Abby didn't touch like that, and she had to be scared, just coming out of her shock. Touching her at all would be too much like taking advantage, and he wasn't about to do that.

Not now. Not ever.

Not when it came to sweet Abby.

Ryan made sure that Julia and Abby were safe in his car, then he removed the car seat from her vehicle, all the while hoping that they were truly okay. Abby was right, the car hadn't been going that fast, and Julia had been buckled in tight. He assumed Abby had been as well. They would be fine, even if Abby was a little stressed out. He didn't blame her, though, not after the accident.

By the time the tow truck arrived, pictures were taken, and everything was in order, Julia was asleep in her car seat in his car, warm and snug like a bug in a rug. Abby had wrung her hands to the point where she probably had a hole in her gloves, but she had stayed strong throughout it all. She was possibly the strongest woman he knew. And considering the women he had in his life, that was saying something.

After everything had been taken care of, they drove in silence to Abby's place, and she even made an appointment for Julia with the pediatrician for the next day.

He knew it was the right course of action, and if Julia had looked the least bit injured or shaken, they would have been at Urgent Care or even the emergency room right then.

They had all missed dinner, but he didn't think he could eat anything. Not when he kept going over what he'd seen in his head. Thoughts of exactly what had happened and what he'd seen with Abby and Julia.

"Do you want to come in for some hot cocoa or something? Or tea?" Abby asked as she lifted Julia into her arms. Ryan worked on getting the car seat out so he could bring it into her house. Someone would have to take her to work the next day. If he did it, then he would just put the car seat back in his vehicle. But Abby had a lot of friends around here, and he assumed she would call one of them to take her.

"You should probably get her to bed." He nodded at Julia.

He didn't miss the disappointment in Abby's gaze, but he knew it likely had nothing to do with him, probably just the fact that she didn't want to be alone. He couldn't blame her. The thought of going back to his big, empty house didn't really settle on his shoulders like it should either.

"I'm going to get her right to sleep, but if you want to come in, at least for a hot drink, you're more than welcome to. I want to say thank you. But I also don't want to take up any more of your time. This has already taken up too much of it."

Ryan shook his head and closed the car door.

"I don't mind. I didn't have any plans. The fact that you guys are safe is all I really need." He paused and thought better of his initial answer. "Yeah, I'll take you up on that hot cocoa, but Adrienne tells me you have something with peppermint."

Abby rolled her eyes and grinned. "She's addicted to that peppermint tea. It's the white chocolate peppermint bark one. I had it last year, as well."

Ryan licked his lips, and he didn't miss the fact that Abby's gaze followed the motion. Apparently, he wasn't the only one that was tired. "I've had it. That was some damn good stuff." He winced, looking down at Julia.

"No worries about the cursing. She's heard worse, even though everyone tries to be good about it. Plus, she's out cold. You're fine."

"Speaking of cold, let's get inside."

"You're right. Standing out here doesn't make a lot of sense. I guess I'm still a little flustered."

He followed her to the house and watched as she deftly opened the door, Julia still in her arms, doing it as if she'd done it a thousand times before. And maybe she had. She had raised Julia alone from birth and hadn't had any real help.

He didn't know how she did it, especially considering he had trouble taking care of himself some days. But she was damn good at it and had even created and ran a whole business on her own. Ryan was just a tattoo artist. Yeah, he was a good one, but he didn't own his own shop. He finally owned his own home, but he didn't have much else.

And...that was enough feeling sorry for himself.

Ryan stood awkwardly in Abby's small living room, setting the car seat down on the floor out of the way as Abby went to put Julia to sleep. He kind of wished he'd been able to say goodnight to the little girl, but that wasn't his place. He was just a friend, and not even a close friend. Maybe over time he and Abby and Julia could get closer, but Abby didn't need him and his troubles.

He didn't need himself and his troubles most days.

Ryan took a look around the space, enjoying the way she had decorated. It looked like a home rather than how his house looked. She had photos on the wall, art and different knickknacks on shelves and tables. The place was clearly childproof as well, with Julia being able to toddle around. But it still felt warm and lived-in. It wasn't dirty, wasn't even messy, but it was clearly a home.

His house, on the other hand, barely had anything on the walls but his TV and a shelf he'd put up so he could set the rest of the entertainment equipment up. He didn't have much in the way of furniture, only what he needed. Honestly, the house was too big for him, but it was a steal since he had worked on revamping and reinstalling things on his own.

But it didn't feel like a home to him. Maybe it should, and probably would later, but for now, he was still working on it. Abby walked out as he was looking at a few photos on the wall, pausing on one in particular.

She must have seen what he was looking at because she came and stood next to him, a small smile on her face. Her eyes didn't look sad, but then again, maybe she was just good at hiding it. After all, he was good at hiding things, too.

"That's Max," Abby said softly.

He swallowed hard. "Julia's father, right?"

"Yes. I try to keep Max around the house for her. And for me, for that matter. I never want to erase him, even though he never got to live in this place."

She didn't seem to mind talking about Max, but he also wasn't going to bring the other man up and hurt her if he didn't need to.

"The place looks great, Abby. I like what you've done with it, and it looks like a perfect home for Julia. You've done well."

She smiled then, her eyes a little brighter. "I've tried. I'm not home that much, not as much as I should be. Between work and making sure Julia gets to see more than just the inside of these walls, I haven't been able to really put the rest of my mark on it."

He snorted. At Abby's look, he explained what he was thinking. "If you could see my place, you'd see why what you just said is hilarious."

"A bachelor pad?"

"Maybe. Or maybe I'm just not good at the whole decorating thing. I'm good with art when it comes to tattoos, but not so much when it comes to my walls."

"You know, one of the Montgomerys would probably help you with that. They're all really good at decorating their houses."

"I've noticed that. But you're pretty great, too."

"Are you offering me a job to decorate your house?"

He just shook his head, smiling. "You never know. In case you have time between tea and Julia and having a life, you may want to decorate a four-bedroom house with way too much space and white walls."

Abby's eyes widened as she led him into the kitchen. "Four bedrooms? Just for you?"

"Yeah, it's ridiculous. I got the house because there was some damage from the last forest fire. The people foreclosed on it before it was even in the middle of that. So I got it at a steal because no one wanted to deal with it. I didn't mind doing the rebuilding because I liked the place and the views. But it's a little too big for me. I probably should just sell it and get something smaller. But I can't quite say goodbye to it."

Abby shook her head as she started melting some chocolate and peppermint bark right into a pan and pulled out the milk. He'd never seen someone actually make hot cocoa that way outside of a movie. His stomach rumbled, and he knew he would have to eat something when he got home.

"Well, I'm sure you'll make it your place. Or you'll sell it if you find that you want to. Or maybe you can rent it out to a family that needs it."

"Maybe. I just don't know yet. But the house works for me."

Abby poured out their hot cocoas and handed him a mug.

He could scent the peppermint and chocolate, and he licked his lips in anticipation. But he didn't take a sip, knowing it would be too hot. "When my parents passed, they left me some money, and I didn't want to just look at it and not have anything to show for what they worked so hard for. I used most of it for investments, but when I saw this place, I had to have it. I donated a lot of the money, but the house? The house is mine, I guess."

"I'm sorry about your parents."

Abby reached out and gripped his arm, giving it a squeeze. He looked down at where she touched him, wondering what it meant. Wondering why he wanted that touch so much. He knew he should leave, knew he'd already overstayed his welcome. But he couldn't go. Not yet.

"They passed a few years ago. The big house may seem like a waste, but it spoke to me. And even though I need to do better about making sure it feels like a home, I think your place is giving me ideas."

She smiled. "Really? It's a two bedroom, but it feels like a one and a half bedroom. Julia has the little half-bedroom that I think used to be an office for someone. I don't know why they made a house this small in this neighborhood, but I think they wanted a little bit of everybody here. Which is good in the long run, but they didn't really think the layout of the house through well. I don't mind it. It's a good starter home for us. Once the business has been up and running for a couple more years, and I feel a little more stable and in the black, I think we'll move. Julia's going to need some space. She's so tiny right now, it's okay, but soon, we're going to be walking all over each other."

"Maybe, but the place still suits you guys pretty well right now."

"Thank you. I love it." They both took sips of their hot chocolates, and he had to hold back an audible moan. He did close his eyes though, and when she let out a soft laugh, he had a feeling she knew exactly what he was thinking.

Well, maybe not exactly since he was thinking about more than the cocoa. He was imagining kissing those lips of hers.

And that's when he knew he had to go.

"This tastes amazing. Thank you."

"Thank you for being there. And thank you for staying. And just...for staying. I know I probably could have handled it on my own, but I'm learning to lean on others, and maybe realizing I don't have to handle everything myself."

They continued drinking their hot cocoa in the kitchen, not even sitting down. He had a feeling if he planned to stay longer, they would have moved into her small living room to talk. But standing in the kitchen felt safer. Safer from what, he didn't know, but just...safer.

He put his empty mug in the sink, filling it up with water to soak. Abby had said she would wash it herself since they weren't dishwasher safe. He didn't understand why things weren't dishwasher safe, but then again, he wasn't going to question it. He'd just had the best peppermint hot cocoa of his life, and with a beautiful woman at that.

He couldn't really complain.

Abby walked him out after explaining to him that she was going to call the Montgomerys and ask for a ride in the morning. It was probably for the best. He didn't work the morning shift, so it wouldn't make sense for him to help out.

But he would have if she'd asked.

And that worried him.

Because he already knew that he wanted to get to know Abby better. And that wasn't good for anyone.

Especially her.

"Thank you for being there, Ryan," she whispered, looking up at him with those big eyes of hers.

He nodded, stuffing his hands into his pockets so he wouldn't reach out and touch her. "I'd say anytime, but I don't really mean anytime."

She smiled again, and he said goodbye, knowing that things would get awkward if he stayed any longer.

By the time he got home, he was exhausted and starving. He could heat up some leftovers from the fridge but knew he should probably cook something since he wanted those leftovers for lunch the next day. He was way too tired for that, though.

He had to work with a few clients at Montgomery Ink Too tomorrow, but then he needed to go to his old shop and try to get his final paycheck. The damn manager hadn't paid him for the last two months he worked there. And it sucked. That was the reason Ryan had quit—well, one of the many reasons. The fact that he got to work with some of the best artists in the country at Montgomery Ink Too now was something big. But the whole non-payment thing with his old boss, even when he had money now, really pissed him the fuck off.

Ryan hadn't always had money. When he left his parents' place, he'd had nothing but the shirt on his back and whatever he had been able to stuff into his bag. They hadn't liked the fact that he didn't want to go to a *real* college. He wanted to go to art school and eventually become a tattoo artist. When he turned eighteen and got his first tattoo—at least waiting until it was legal—his parents had thrown a fit. They kicked him out, called him names, and then blamed him for his twin.

Ryan didn't need the guilt trip from his parents regarding Michael. He already blamed himself enough.

And if he really thought about it, Ryan knew that his twin would fuck things up again. His brother was the reason Ryan had been fired from three of his last four jobs. The only reason he hadn't been fired from his previous one was because he quit before that happened. Ryan knew that if Michael had shown up there, he would have ended up losing that position just like he had lost everything else.

So now, the only things Ryan had were this house, his new job with the Montgomerys, and the money his parents had left him out of guilt.

They had tried to get ahold of him, tried to be in his life again, but it had always been on their terms, following their rules, and for their needs.

They hadn't liked his decisions. Didn't seem to like *him*.

But in the end, they hadn't liked Michael even more.

And though they had loved Michael, and though they had put all of their attention into making sure Michael was cared for and loved, they had made mistakes.

And that was how Michael ended up the way he was now.

And that was why Ryan was the way *he* was.

Ryan quickly heated up his food, knowing he would just go to the bakery the next day for his lunch, and tried to let the stress from the day drain from him. He didn't like thinking about his family. Honestly, he didn't like thinking about most things that hurt. He had his empty house with its bare walls and knew that would have to be enough for now.

There was no use thinking about Abby and her warm home or the little girl that made him smile.

He was just about to wash his dishes when someone knocked on the front door.

No one really knew where he lived. Those at Montgomery Ink Too had his address on file, but knowing his day, Ryan had a feeling he knew exactly who was on the other side of the door.

And exactly what they wanted.

So, when he opened the door and found his twin there, he didn't sigh. He wasn't even surprised.

Michael was back.

And that meant things were about to get fucked up.

Again.

Chapter Three

Abby wasn't having the best of days. It wasn't as bad as the night before, but it still wasn't that great. Thea had come by the house to pick her up and take her and Julia to the pediatrician. Her friend had offered as soon as Abby called to tell her what had happened. Abby didn't even have to ask for help.

The fact that she'd planned to ask in the first place meant that she was getting better at it. Or at least taking that first step. Julia was fine, not even a bruise or a bump. But it never hurt to be careful.

Abby hadn't slept at all the night before and had just lain in her own bed with Julia wrapped up beside her, sleeping. The fact that her baby girl could sleep so well after everything that had happened at least made her feel a little bit better. Julia hadn't been scared, and in reality, the accident hadn't been that bad. Abby had probably hurt herself more falling on ice, and *had* hurt herself more that way now that she thought about it.

The morning at the pediatrician's had taken time out of her day. Julia was now at the babysitter's—not with the Montgomerys since Abby hadn't had the time or the brain power to ask about that yet. But she would do it soon, though maybe not today since she was still trying to catch up with everything else.

Abby owned the teashop on her own and didn't have any help, so Thea had sent over one of her workers to help Abby and open the store for her. Abby was so grateful, but she hadn't been able to actually voice the words with as much emotion as she wanted to. She knew she had to hire someone to help her, and that was in the plans for the next quarter. The fact that she couldn't take any time off for her daughter without closing the store meant that things needed to change.

She hadn't been able to even think about doing that during the first months of her business, but now, things were different.

They had to be.

And speaking of different, she couldn't help but think of Ryan.

She held back a groan.

He had been in the right place at the right time, and she knew that they lived close to one another, but she hadn't known there was a chance that he could be exactly what she needed him to be. He'd calmed her down and hadn't said anything that might've put the blame on her. Of course, it hadn't been her fault. She'd been driving at precisely the correct speed, but her mind still kept going to what could have happened if things had gone differently.

Or if things had gotten worse.

Ryan had been there for her, had shared hot chocolate with her, and...had given her a look that worried her. Not one where she thought he meant her harm, but one that indicated there might be something between them.

Maybe she was thinking too hard about it. Her system was already on overload thinking about her daughter and the accident. But every time Abby looked at Ryan, every time she thought of him, she couldn't help but wonder why her mind went to him in the way it did.

There was just something about him that drew her to him. She shouldn't be drawn in, not with how their friends were all connected.

She and Ryan were friends, and all of their friends were friends. He worked close to her and lived even closer. Having anything more than what they currently had was a recipe for disaster.

But it didn't help that she just couldn't get him off her mind.

Her sleepless night had been spent lying in bed, holding Julia close, not only thinking about the accident but also thinking about Ryan and the way that he looked at her and tried to take care of her.

The bell over the door rang, and she looked up to see Adrienne walking in, a smile on her face.

"How are you feeling, babe?" Adrienne hugged her close but then took a step back. Abby was still getting used to the way the Montgomerys touched, the way they were constantly hugging and making sure that the people around them knew that they were cared for and thought of.

The Gallaghers and Max had been the same way. Max was always holding her, brushing her hair away from her face. He was constantly touching her, showing her that he loved her.

She missed him with every passing hour and thought of him every single day. She would think about him for the rest of her life, regardless if she went on dates with other people, no matter that she was thinking about Ryan.

Max would always be a part of her. Trying to find out who she was in this new life of hers had already taken its toll.

"Okay, what are you thinking about?" Adrienne moved closer, and Abby could hear the worry in the other woman's voice.

Abby shook her head, organizing the tea canisters in front of her. "Nothing. Or maybe too much."

"Is Julia okay? Are you?"

"She's fine. A little hyper since I let her have too much sugar this morning because I was feeling bad."

Adrienne snorted and then leaned across the counter. "Daisy is the same way sometimes. I think I spoil her more than Mace does, and that's saying something."

"Daisy is anything but spoiled." Daisy was Mace's daughter from a previous relationship, and she'd just started living with Mace full-time after Daisy's mom left. Now that Adrienne was in Mace's life as more than just a friend, that meant that Adrienne and Daisy spent their days together now. Abby liked the way the new family seemed to be working, even though they were going slow to make sure that Daisy was happy.

But that little girl was perfect. Just like Abby's daughter.

"I'm okay." Abby said the words again, mostly to convince herself, but Adrienne just looked at her.

"And if it's not the accident, why wouldn't you be okay? What were you thinking about when I walked in?"

There was something about the way the Montgomery girls spoke to her that always pulled Abby out of her shell. They weren't harsh, they didn't push. But they were always there. Abby was never alone when it came to the Montgomerys. She knew she should be grateful, and she was, but she wasn't sure how she could say these next words.

"I was just thinking about Max."

Pity didn't enter Adrienne's eyes, and for that, Abby was grateful. There was a deep sadness there, though. And even though Adrienne had never met Max, she had heard enough about him over the last few months to know where Abby was at emotionally. Or at least where she had been before last night.

"Do you want to talk about him? Or anything? I don't have a client for another hour, so we could sip some tea and just talk."

Abby looked around, noting that while the store might be empty, she had a few online orders that she needed to take care of. But she could take ten minutes to talk with her friend. She could use those ten minutes to try and get her thoughts in order.

"I'd like that. But can we just stand out here if that's okay? I want to be sure I'm here in case a customer walks in."

"I get it. Ryan and Shep are over at the shop taking care of their own clients. Mace is coming in later, but he's on kid duty today."

"You know, speaking of kid duty…"

Adrienne's eyes widened, and then she clapped her hands, bouncing from one foot to the other. "Have we worn you down? I knew we would."

Abby rolled her eyes. "If it's okay with you, I'd like to be worked into the schedule. Especially this next quarter once I hire someone to actually help me at the shop."

"I can't wait. We'll work with spreadsheets. Not that I'm the best with spreadsheets, but Roxie and Shea are really good at them."

As accountants, Shea and Roxie had heads for numbers and schedules. If they could help Abby with trying to make sure she did as much as possible without running herself ragged, then she'd take it.

"So…" Adrienne began. "What's going on?"

"I loved Max. I still love him. I'm going to love him forever. It's just hard trying to figure out exactly how I'm supposed to feel when, sometimes, I just want to say it's okay to *not* feel."

"I've never gone through what you have, so I can't really tell you what to feel. But then again, even if I had been through it, I wouldn't tell you what to feel. If you want to miss Max and still move on? I think you know what you're doing with that. And I like the man that I've learned through you, and the way you talk about him around Julia. I think he would have wanted you to figure out this new person you are."

Abby smiled, stirring her tea. They had gone with an herbal, fruit-infused tea that was a little too summery for the season, but she'd needed to think about something a little peppier than the cool winter.

"I've dated. Well, I've been on two dates. I didn't wear my ring. I couldn't. I didn't even get married, so I only have the engagement ring to begin with. We were waiting for Julia to be born before we got married."

"I know, you told me. And I love that ring. I'm glad you keep it in your tray on your desk."

"That way, it's always with me at work. I used to keep it in my wallet, but then my wallet got too heavy, and it hurt to think of. I keep it here, and then I take it home with me. I don't know why I do that, but I'll find a pattern that works for me. I'm never going to forget him. And I don't want to. But it's just…it's just weird starting over."

"And is there someone that you want to start over with?" Adrienne's question was probing, but it wasn't malicious. They were just two girlfriends talking about what-ifs in relationships. Abby hadn't done that in forever, hadn't allowed herself to. Maybe it was time she tried.

"Not really. I just…I don't know. It's just a little hard." She wasn't going to tell Adrienne about Ryan yet. Or ever. Those were just weird thoughts that didn't have anything to do with anything anyway.

Just because she had felt heat between them, some kind of connection, it didn't mean that she should be up in arms in her head trying to figure out exactly where she stood with him, and what her thoughts with Max would be if she thought of Ryan more.

"Well, whenever you want to talk, I'm here for you. All of us are. And we love you. Because you're family now, even if you don't really understand yet that the Montgomerys take over your life and never let you go."

They both laughed at that, and Abby rolled her eyes. When they finished their tea, Adrienne left to get back to work. Abby finished up her online orders and then helped a few customers who came in to shop for the holidays. Over the next two hours, Abby moved right into lunch. Teas'd was full of people. The holiday rush was nice, and she knew that her bank ledgers would be happy after today.

Abby was just finishing up the last of the rush, thinking that she would probably grab something quick to eat over at Thea's, when Ryan walked in, his hands in his pockets, and his leather jacket zipped up to ward off the cold from outside.

She was so surprised to see him, she nearly dropped her tea canister. She shouldn't be shocked. He came in often for tea, especially since he had coffee in the morning over at Thea's and then enjoyed afternoon tea with her.

She didn't know why, but she couldn't stop looking at his eyes.

She really should stop looking at his eyes.

"Hey, I just wanted to check in on you. See if you were okay. Adrienne said Thea took you and Julia over to the pediatrician's and that Julia is fine. But I didn't know if you went to the doctor, too."

Abby set the tea canister down on the counter, grateful that she didn't break it open, but a little annoyed that she didn't have anything to do with her hands. "I didn't go, but I'm not bruised. I don't even have a seat belt burn. We were going so slow, I think I've hurt myself more running into the couch."

Ryan's lips quirked into a smile. "I've broken a toe running into a couch, so I get it."

Abby cringed. "Me, too. It's those damn pinky toes. They just like to latch on."

She was talking about toes. Broken toes.

Apparently, she was rusty at this. Whatever *this* was.

"Yeah, pretty much. But I'm glad to see you're okay. And I'm glad Julia is, too. I could use some tea if that's okay with you."

Abby jumped into action, moving around the counter and closer to him. "I'm so sorry, I should've asked. What can I get you?"

"You don't have to serve me, Abby. I'm just here because I like your company. And I like your tea."

Her stomach did that weird flopping thing that she hadn't felt in so long, and she was kind of worried about it. What was she doing? Was she reading this wrong? Or maybe she was going insane and just thinking too much. Because Ryan was her friend. Nothing more.

She just had to get that through her head.

"What are you thinking about, Abby?" Ryan leaned forward, his hands still in his pockets. He didn't touch her, but she could still feel the heat of him. "You look like you're thinking hard. Are you okay?"

She paused. "Are you saying that thinking hard will hurt my head?"

Ryan blinked and then threw his head back and laughed. She really liked that laugh. It was deep, and a little rough.

And she really needed to stop thinking about *rough*.

"No, that's not what I meant. But, apparently, I ramble when it comes to you."

"I don't think you rambled. But maybe that's because I ramble even more than you."

"See? You think I ramble if you said 'even more.'"

Abby put her hands over her face and let out a tiny scream. "I think we need to start over on this conversation."

"No, I don't mind. But I really could use some tea."

She nodded, letting out a breath. "I have that peppermint that you like. The one without the chocolate."

"I love the one with the chocolate, but for some reason, I do like the other one more."

She quickly got to work steeping it as he looked around the shop, gazing at each of the gift baskets she had made. She kept her eyes on him rather than her hands, and was grateful she was a pro at this, or she probably would have burned herself.

When it was done, she poured herself a cup as well, not knowing why since she'd had enough tea for the day. But she didn't want him to drink alone.

"Here you go." His hands brushed hers as he took the cup from her, his gaze meeting hers, as well.

She swallowed hard, wondering why she felt like this. Why there was a fluttering in her stomach and in her chest.

Ryan was just her friend. They had done this countless times before.

It shouldn't feel like this.

But it did.

"Thank you." A pause. "Would you like to go out with me sometime?"

And then his eyes grew wide, and he set down his tea. "I didn't mean to ask that."

That sharp stabbing sensation in her chest hurt more than she thought it would at his words. At the fact he hadn't wanted to be with her…had thought it a mistake? Just after one moment of clarity?

Ouch.

She stood there, blinking, then looked up at him.

"Oh? I see."

Ryan cursed under his breath and then moved around the counter. He cupped her face. He'd never touched her like this before. And it made her freeze.

He was touching her, his hands soft. He was caring. And he was touching her.

"I didn't mean it like that, I swear. I only meant that I didn't mean to ask you out like that. The thoughts were going through my head, and I didn't realize the words had spilled out until they did."

"So, do you want to take it back?"

He was silent for so long that she was afraid she might cry. Even with his hands still on her face. She didn't know why she felt like this with rejection.

But she did.

"I didn't know what you were going to say. So I didn't ask before. And I didn't want to take advantage of our friendship by asking. But now that I did, I don't want to take it back."

"Oh." Her words a breath.

"So? Abby? Do you want to get some dinner with me?" He ran his thumb across her cheek, and she barely resisted closing her eyes and leaning into him. "Any time you want. Any place. All you have to do is say yes, and I'm yours."

That sounded nice. Being his. Though she didn't know what that would entail.

And she knew she was ready, but she didn't know exactly what that meant.

Because she took so long to answer, she saw his gaze shutter, saw the way he wanted to move back. He thought she was going to say no. He wondered if he was making a mistake.

And because she knew she should say no, because their friendship was more important than anything, she did the one thing that she shouldn't do.

She opened her mouth and spoke. "Yes. I'd love to go out with you."

She just hoped she hadn't made another mistake.

Chapter Four

Ryan had lost his damn mind, and it wasn't even one in the afternoon yet. He'd left Abby in her shop, not even touching his tea since it seemed awkward to stay after she'd said yes to the date he knew neither of them expected.

He'd just looked at her there and hadn't been able to hold himself back. He liked her, that much he knew. But with his brother back in town, it was kind of hard to think about anything but the fact that a calamity was probably on its way.

He had no right to step into Abby's life like he was, but apparently, he couldn't help himself.

He thought about her often—the way she smiled, the way sadness sometimes shone in her eyes before she shook it off. She didn't ignore it, that much he could see, but she tried to move forward.

He understood that. He tried to do the same. He just figured that Abby was a little more successful at it than he was.

Of course, her memory stared at her every day in the eyes of her daughter.

His came back and asked for money, asked for a place to stay, and tried to find ways to ruin Ryan's life.

Because Michael always wanted to discover ways to get into Ryan's mind, figure out how to get under his brother's skin. Because Ryan's twin wasn't a good man. No matter how hard Ryan wished it were different.

"What's up with you, man?" Shep asked from his station. Ryan turned to his friend and watched as the man cleaned the area. Shep had just finished a tattoo, and the client had already left. Ryan figured that his boss had a few minutes before he either went to check on his daughter, Livvy, or took the next walk-in client. Even with the holiday season, they were busier than usual.

Montgomery Ink Too was a branch of the Montgomery Ink franchise that was settled in downtown Denver. The artists at the original Montgomery Ink had waiting lists that were months long, but they also had room for some walk-ins for last-minute tattoo decisions that meant something important.

Since Shep and Adrienne had modeled Montgomery Ink Too after the one up in Denver, and their cousins were also investors, it made sense that the shop would be like the other. Montgomery Ink Too wasn't as busy as the original one, but it was getting busier as the months passed. They were getting a reputation for having talented artists and a damn good business practice.

That meant that while Ryan had a long list of people waiting for him, he was also able to take walk-ins just like the rest of them. He did his best to make sure everyone got exactly what they wanted and turned away clients that wanted something he couldn't give.

Most of the time, that happened with women who wanted to get to know him better, or even men who wanted to get to know him like that. Yes, he was bisexual and had dated some of his clients back in the day, but he'd learned the hard way not to do ink for anyone that he wanted to sleep with.

Things got tricky with that. Of course, when it came to Ryan's relationships, everything was complicated.

"Hey, you there?" Shep asked. "What are you thinking about that's making you look like you're going insane?"

Ryan flipped him off. "I don't look like that."

"I beg to differ. But what's up?"

"I asked Abby out." He hadn't meant to blurt it out like that, but apparently, he hadn't been able to hold it back.

He hadn't been able to hold a lot of himself back lately.

That didn't bode well for his dates—or his life, for that matter. Considering that Michael could pop out again at any moment, Ryan really wasn't sure what might happen next.

Now was not the time to be dating a woman that he really admired, respected, and one that happened to have a daughter that he really liked.

"You asked out Abby?" Adrienne asked as she walked through the door, Mace behind her.

Ryan put his hands over his face and shook his head. "Why did you have to walk in at that exact moment?"

Adrienne just grinned. "Because I'm amazing and I needed to hear this, apparently. So, did she say yes?" She shook her head. "Of course she said yes. You wouldn't look so sick to your stomach if she hadn't said yes."

Mace looked down at his woman and then back up at Ryan. "I have no idea what that means. Why do you look sick?"

"Because she said yes." Ryan let his hands fall and stared at his friends. They were in a lull between projects, something that they all liked to take advantage of if they had time. Having moments where they could discuss business and life was good for the four of them.

However, Ryan really wanted someone to walk into the shop right now so he could work on a tattoo. Anything so he didn't have to talk to Adrienne about the fact that he had asked Abby on a date. Anything so he didn't have to talk about any of it at all.

But because this was Ryan and his life, no one walked in.

He turned to face Adrienne fully. "She said yes," he repeated. "Yes. What was she thinking? What was *I* thinking? I wasn't supposed to ask her out. I know the rules. You don't poach on your own territory. Or someone else's territory. I can't even make words anymore. What is wrong with me?" He put his head in his hands again, ignoring the way that Shep and Mace started chuckling beside him.

He would get them back later for this. Of course, he had already gotten to Mace a bit when Mace started dating Adrienne. He'd even walked in on them once—or three times. He'd lost count. He really didn't want to think about that.

Shep had come into Ryan's life already married with a baby. But Ryan had also walked in on Shep and Shea making out in the closet like teenagers.

Apparently, his lot in life was to walk in on his friends making out with their people.

He really needed a new role.

Or a new life.

Or maybe a new address.

Could he live in Timbuktu? Was that even a place anymore?

Oh, God, he was losing his mind.

Adrienne stood in front of him then, and he looked down at her. She pulled her dark hair back, her bright eyes staring at him. "You asked her because you like her. She said yes because she likes you. She's gentle, but then again, Ryan, so are you." Ryan opened his mouth to protest, to say there wasn't anything gentle about him and they all knew it, but Adrienne held up her hands. "No. You are. You might be a badass like everyone else here. You have the tattoos, the piercings, you have the bad attitude when you feel like it. But you're sweet. And I don't exactly know why you are so sweet sometimes because you won't tell us anything about your life, but I will wait for gossip a little bit later. What I want to know now is if you're happy about this. Because I see something in your eyes, and it looks like fear. Do you want to talk about it?"

"Don't make him talk if he doesn't want to," Shep murmured.

"Don't tell your sister what to do, it'll just make her go off in the opposite direction," Mace answered.

Adrienne flipped off her brother and her man, all while looking at Ryan. That took skill.

"I asked her out. I don't know if I should have."

"I've watched you look at her, just like I've watched her look at you. I like the two of you. And I know that you both respect each other and our little territory here, as you put it, enough that you're not going to make the same mistakes you might have with other people. Go slow. Test it out. Just know if you make mistakes and hurt her, I will geld you. I'll still let you work here, but you will have no balls. That's not a threat as your employer but as a friend of Abby's. And as your friend. Don't go ball-less, Ryan. Treasure your balls. Don't piss me off. And don't hurt Abby."

Both Shep and Mace crossed their legs, laughter in their eyes. Ryan flipped them off just because he could and then looked down at Adrienne once more.

"You sure do like to talk about my balls."

"That's my sister, you asshole," Shep put in.

"And my woman. Maybe I'll be the one to geld you before you go see Abby. She might not like it if you have no balls."

Everyone started laughing, and Ryan closed his eyes, holding back a groan. He'd officially lost his mind, but then again, he couldn't really help it. He hadn't grown up in the sanest family, not with his parents doing their best to make sure that Michael was the most spoiled brat ever. Not when they had put all of their hopes and dreams into Ryan and then pushed him away when he didn't do what he was supposed to.

"Why don't you tell me what else is going on while I clean up my station and get ready for my client?"

"It's fine."

"Never say that, dude," Mace put in, going to his station after he'd kissed his girl. "That means something is really going on, and Adrienne will find out. Never mess with the Montgomerys."

"I think my mom cross-stitched that on a pillow once," Shep said with a laugh.

"You know, that doesn't really surprise me," Ryan said, setting up his station as well. They each had an appointment within the next thirty minutes, so as they got to work, the subject was thankfully changed—but only for a few moments. Too soon, Adrienne was right back, asking the same question.

"What's wrong, Ryan?"

"My brother's back in town."

They didn't know about his brother, and from the looks on their faces, they didn't know why his brother being in town was an issue. But it wasn't like he could really keep the secret because he couldn't hide anything from them.

They were really good at their jobs.

And he wasn't talking about being tattoo artists.

"And? What's wrong with that?" Adrienne asked. She paused and looked at him directly. "I mean, there has to be something wrong with it, or you wouldn't be as worried as you are. But can you explain? Or is this something that is best done over beers when we're not at work and waiting for someone to walk in at any moment. I'm not going to pry." She glared at her man and her brother as they snickered. "I don't pry when it's really important. Or I guess, I don't pry if it'll hurt, even if it's still important. You know that."

"I do," Ryan whispered. Both Shep and Mace agreed, nodding and verbalizing their assent. At least, that was something.

"My brother's a drug addict."

Adrienne reached out for Ryan, and he didn't pull back when she patted his hand. She immediately dropped her arm, though, and he was grateful. He didn't mind being touched, but it was hard enough to talk about this subject without having to worry about hurting his friend's feelings.

"And is he using right now?" Mace asked.

Ryan nodded, thankful for the question. Just because someone was an addict didn't mean they were using all the time. You could be completely sober, going on a decade of not using, and still be an addict. You would always have that craving. Ryan wasn't an addict, but his twin was. And that meant he had seen the signs, had attended the classes, had gone to the support groups. He had tried to help his brother his entire life. But he hadn't been enough.

That was why he needed to stay away from Abby.

But he knew he wouldn't.

Because maybe he was an asshole.

"He's using again. He showed up on my doorstep last night after I got back from Abby's. I was making sure she got home okay. He wanted money, wanted a place to stay. But I had to push him away. I have my damn house because of the money my parents left to me out of guilt." He paused. "I had to push him away."

"Guilt?" Adrienne asked.

Ryan shook his head as the bell on top of the door rang. Mace's client had arrived. "I'll talk about it later. Promise. But I'm not going to hurt Abby. I can't. Because if I do, I'm going to hate myself more than I already do."

Adrienne gave him a look, and he knew this conversation wasn't over. But it wasn't like he could talk right then. He had so many thoughts going through his mind, and was too busy thinking about Abby and Michael and Julia. He knew he should stay away, but he wasn't going to.

Thankfully, his client came in next, so he didn't have to think about anything personal anymore.

He only had to think about the ink. Just had to concentrate on the art that he was about to create, the piece that would conform exactly to what it needed to be and would be a representation of what his client needed, what they wanted.

This was something he could do.

This was something he was damn good at.

And maybe, just maybe, he wouldn't fuck up everything else.

"You think Carter's okay?" Landon asked from across Ryan's bedroom.

"Well, he went home with Roxie, so I guess he's as okay as he's going to be right now." Ryan looked in his closet and then glanced over at his friend.

Landon and Ryan were still new friends, but they were close. They'd met through Mace and then Shep and hadn't looked back. They had beers with the guys sometimes and, considering they hadn't married into the Montgomerys like the rest of them, they had formed a bond.

They were not dating, contrary to popular belief. It amazed Ryan how many people thought that the suave and suited broker would want anything to do with Ryan in his jeans and usually ratty shirt, with all his piercings and tattoos.

But Ryan didn't mind. Landon was hot, and he was also one of Ryan's best friends. He and Landon had never dated, and considering that he knew that Landon's gaze had settled on another of their friends, a certain art teacher with a penchant for glaring at them both, Ryan was glad they hadn't.

Plus, Ryan had always had eyes for Abby. Landon had noticed that from the start, even if it had taken a little bit longer for everyone else to see it.

"I can't believe that Carter got burned as bad as he did at Thea's bakery," Landon said, shaking his head. "I swear, between the tattoo shop getting broken into, and the bakery having a freaking explosion, it's like one thing after another with the Montgomerys."

"Truer words have never been spoken," Ryan said, turning with two shirts in his hands. "The dark blue or the black?"

Landon raised a brow, shaking his head. "They're the exact same shirt. Just in two different colors."

Ryan shrugged. "You say that as if you don't own eighteen of the same shirt."

Landon put his hand on his chest as if wounded, and Ryan rolled his eyes. He knew that Landon was trying to jokingly come on to him because it was safe. The two of them were friends for a reason.

"You're an idiot. I'm just going to say it now. You're an idiot."

"No, Ryan, my dear boy, you're the idiot. And you want to wear the other black one you have. The one that I gave you for your birthday."

"That shirt? No. That shirt cost more than I make in a month."

Landon rolled his eyes and pushed Ryan out of the way. "No, not so much. And I know what Adrienne and Shep pay you and what you make from your clients. You make a hell of a lot more in a week than I paid for that shirt. I got it on sale. I like money. Therefore, I don't spend it unless I have to. Remember?"

Ryan huffed out a breath and then stripped off his current shirt before putting on the one that Landon handed over.

"See? I was right. It looks the best. And make sure you brush your hair and put in some of that gel you like. I already know that you've already taken care of your facial hair. You take care of your beard more than you take care of anything else on you or in this house."

Ryan ran his hand over his beard and grinned. "It takes a lot of work to make this look good."

Landon burst out laughing. "Are you saying you don't look good unless you put work into it?"

Ryan flipped him off. "Oh, shut up. Beard care is some of the most important care you can do. It takes a lot of soaps and oils to make sure it smells nice and isn't a Petri dish of crap that you don't want to think about."

"Emphasis on the crap."

Ryan snorted since that was true. He and his friends who had beards took care of themselves, unlike some of the guys out there who grew a beard and ignored it. Didn't they ever want their mouths on another person? If they did, they needed to take care of their damn beards.

Ryan went to brush his hair like Landon had told him to. His friend was better at this whole dating thing than Ryan was, so he would take the other man's advice.

"But back to Carter," Ryan began, "he's going to be okay. As for if he and Roxie are going to be okay together? That's a whole other story."

Landon sighed, leaning against the doorway between the master bathroom and the master bath. "I know. I'm a little worried about those two. I don't think they're going to last. I don't think they can."

Ryan met Landon's gaze in the mirror. "Do you know something I don't?"

Landon shook his head. "No, I don't. I just have a feeling. But maybe Carter getting hurt like he did will force the two of them to actually talk to one another. Talking's hard. People say it's easy, then they yell at each other for not talking when it's important. But actually coming up with the words and trying to figure out what you feel? That's a lot harder than it should be."

Ryan glanced at his friend. He wasn't sure if Landon was talking about Roxie and Carter or him and Kaylee, but it wasn't like Ryan could ask. As his friend had said, talking was hard. And he wasn't about to broach that subject when Landon wasn't ready—or when Ryan had to think about Abby.

"Has Michael stopped by again?" Landon asked, seemingly out of the blue.

Ryan shook his head. "I haven't seen him since he came by last night." His brother had stopped by two other times over the past week, and Ryan had pushed him away each time. He hated doing it, but he knew it was for the best.

Ryan had almost ended up in jail once because of Michael, and he wasn't going to do it again. There was only one way to help his brother, and that was by making sure that Michael saw and confronted his own demons. Every time he came for food or money and Ryan gave in, Ryan ended up hurt, and Michael ended up in a worse downward spiral. Ryan had attempted to get Michael counseling, but he'd refused. He'd tried to get him treatment, and Michael had almost beaten Ryan to death.

There was nothing Ryan could do except try to protect his own life and pray that, no matter what happened, Michael would land on his feet.

Because he always did.

"I just hope he doesn't somehow find me on my date with Abby."

Landon narrowed his eyes. "It's not going to happen. I know that you've already had to push your brother away numerous times, but you might have to do it again if he comes after you with her. I'm just saying."

"I know. And it sucks. But I'm going on a date with a woman I respect and admire. And now I want to throw up because if I fuck this up, I'll never forgive myself."

"You're not going to fuck this up."

"You know Abby, Landon. She's soft. She's gentle. And she's been through hell and back. I can't believe she said yes."

"She said yes because you're a catch. Because you're a good man, and you're not as rough-and-tumble as you think. She said yes because she likes you. And if you both go slow, if you are as gentle as you think she is, you'll be fine."

"You're not going to threaten my balls like the rest of them did?" Ryan said with a laugh.

"I want nothing to do with your balls, Ryan. Contrary to what others think, I really don't care for that particular part of your anatomy."

Ryan threw a hand towel at Landon and then laughed. He needed his friends. Because sometimes, he felt like he was all alone, staring into an abyss full of the answers to the problems he had made for himself. He knew that Michael wasn't gone forever. His parents might be, their decisions forever weighing on him, but Michael would be back.

Though for now, he was going to push those thoughts to the side.

Because tonight was about him and Abby.

Tonight was about another first. And no matter what, he wasn't going to fuck it up.

Chapter Five

Abby answered the door after the first ring and almost swallowed her tongue at the sight before her. Ryan looked hot.

Of course she'd known he was hot, especially considering that she hadn't been able to take her eyes off of him whenever he walked into a room.

But tonight he wore dark jeans and a black button-up, all under a thick leather jacket.

It might be cold outside, but it was sure hot in here.

Apparently, her mind was now making really bad jokes, but she couldn't really help herself.

"You look amazing," Ryan said softly. "Seriously amazing."

She smiled and looked down at herself. She wore tall, knee-high black boots over her thick tights that were a criss-cross plaid. Then she had on a nice knitted wrap dress that showcased her curves but not so much that she felt self-conscious. She'd left her hair down in soft waves that had actually taken her a while to get right.

Her hair was sort of a fluffy mess if she didn't handle it in just the right way. It was either not curly enough or too curly. Other days, it was a little straight, a little flat, or a mix of everything all at once.

So she had spent some time getting ready, trying to make sure that she didn't look like a complete crazy woman when she went on her date.

Ryan didn't seem to mind her hair or her curves, considering that she had a good amount of cleavage in this dress.

Not too much, and not too little. Just right.

Apparently, she was going to be running Goldilocks through her head during this date.

Yes, she'd dated since Max, but those two times didn't really count in her head. They hadn't lasted more than the one date each, and she definitely didn't have the same butterflies she did now.

Why was she doing this again?

Ryan smiled at her. *Oh yeah, that's why.*

"You look nice yourself," she said, her voice far too breathy. "I just need to get my bag and my jacket."

"No problem. Is Julia in tonight? Or is she off at the babysitter's?"

Abby sucked in a breath when Ryan helped her with her coat, his breath warm on the back of her neck. He'd moved her hair out of the way so he could slide her jacket over her shoulders, and she tried not to shiver at his touch or nearness.

This was just a first date. She knew Ryan. They were friends.

She didn't have to freak out about this.

But, apparently, that was exactly what she was going to do.

"She's at Mace and Adrienne's. Shep and Shea offered since Livvy and Julia are like best friends now, but Adrienne sort of drove over and kidnapped my daughter."

Ryan snorted, shaking his head.

Abby grabbed her bag, smiling as well. "I know, the Montgomerys are a little bit insane."

"But that's why we love them." She locked up behind herself and then walked out to Ryan's car, letting him close the door behind her, even though she could have done it herself.

She kind of liked being taken care of, but maybe that was because it was Ryan. He and the Montgomerys didn't try to take care of her in a way that said they thought she couldn't do it on her own.

They just wanted to help. And like she'd said before, she was doing better at accepting that help. Even if it was one small step at a time. Of course, she was just going to have to keep thinking of life as one step at a time if she didn't want to fall in love herself. It was easier said than done.

"So I didn't actually ask where we're going. All you said was to dress nicely casual, which is not that helpful."

Ryan laughed. "Yeah, sorry about that. I was picking between two different places, seeing which one would need a reservation."

"A reservation? Look at you, getting all fancy."

He grinned at her as he pulled out of the driveway. "I can't help it.

I'm just the kind of fancy guy you think I am."

She glanced at the tattoos peeking out from the cuff at his wrist and figured, yes, he was just as fancy as he needed to be.

"Anyway, we're going down to that new Italian place. Mace said he and Adrienne really like it, and they don't take reservations. But I called ahead, just to make sure there wasn't that long of a wait. So we're good right now. There was another place that's more like a deli that I figured you might like, but they did need reservations."

Abby shook her head. Colorado Springs was growing by leaps and bounds with each passing day. New people, higher-priced homes, and new restaurants made the city feel like it was booming, even if it still felt like the place she had come to when she needed to heal. She just wondered what it would feel like in a couple more years when they were out of space and all that was left were people and the mountains they could see everywhere they looked.

"I've been to that deli place, it's not really a deli. It's more like a harvest area where they try to tell you exactly how homegrown and farm-to-table all of the meals are. In detail."

Ryan grinned, getting onto the highway. "Yeah, I know. Good food, but even with the reservations, I wasn't sure that you really wanted a lecture before our date."

"Well, at least it would give us something to talk about if things got awkward."

There was silence.

Well…speaking of awkward.

"You know, I didn't think of that. Maybe I should have made reservations."

She pushed at his arm, and he grinned over his shoulder as he turned off the highway. "You're mean."

"You're the one who brought up awkwardness. But, I figured we're friends first, right? And if we can't figure out something to talk about, we can always bring up the Montgomerys or Julia. Or keep stuffing our faces full of food so we don't actually have to think about it."

"I like that idea. Although I might gain ten pounds tonight if I get too nervous."

Ryan parked and looked over her body. "You know, I'd be okay with that. Or you staying just the way you are." He winced. "I was trying to say that you look hot, but I feel like I sort of mansplained to you about your own body. Please ignore me."

She shook her head, laughing as she undid her seatbelt. "Well, at least we're starting the awkward talk early."

Ryan just shook his head as the two of them got out of the car and she met him around the front. He took her hand then, and she smiled. "Okay?" he asked.

"Okay." And it was okay. Just because this was a first date didn't mean that she had to overthink every single movement. Because, in the end, no matter what, Abby still wanted to remain Ryan's friend. Even if this all turned to hell, and their chemistry really was just friendship with a touch of butterflies? She wanted him in her life.

She'd already lost enough, and she didn't want to forfeit the friendship she'd already made.

Ryan squeezed her hand as they walked into the restaurant. "Abby? You doing all right?"

She nodded. "Yeah, just getting a little too introspective. Ignore me."

"The problem is, Abby, I can't ignore you."

She swallowed hard as they followed the hostess to their table. Ryan said all the right things at the right times. She couldn't help but wonder why she couldn't seem to do the same.

She didn't know what to say to him to explain that she really did enjoy his company. Maybe she should just say those words out loud, but she didn't want to scare him.

She was really bad at this. She always had been. It was a wonder that Max had taken to her at all.

And…she should probably stop thinking about Max since she was on a date.

"So, do you have any food allergies I should worry about?"

Abby shook her head at Ryan's question. "No, although I probably shouldn't eat a whole bowl of pasta. Maybe I should add a veggie or some protein to it."

"True, although I could probably eat a whole bowl of pasta right now. I think I was too nervous to eat all day." Ryan winced, shaking his head. "Forget I said that. Pretend I'm all manly and confident and know what I'm doing."

Abby grinned, sipping her water. "Thank God. Because I feel like I have no idea what I'm doing."

"Yay, that makes two of us. Should make for some rousing conversation."

"And if we do get that big bowl of pasta, it means we can eat more when things get awkward."

Ryan raised his water glass in a toast, and she laughed. Maybe they could do this. After all, they were just Ryan and Abby. Friends.

And totally not freaking out, even if they were doing it together.

Maybe. "So, how was work?" Ryan asked.

They had already given their orders to the waiter and were now sipping on a nice house red wine. It was part of happy hour, thankfully. She knew that both she and Ryan liked to save their money. And she knew that Ryan would only have one glass, considering that he'd already told her as much. She only wanted one glass as well because she needed to keep her wits about her. Plus, she wanted to make sure that when she went to pick up Julia later, she wasn't completely intoxicated.

Being a single mom wasn't easy, but she was figuring it out.

At least, she hoped she was.

The food came, and she dug into her scallop linguine. She didn't usually go for seafood, but it sounded amazing. Ryan got the chicken piccata with a little side of Alfredo. The fact that he had gotten an extra side of pasta just made them both laugh.

"It's really for both of us," he said once the waiter had left. "Just in case we say something stupid and need to stuff our faces with pasta."

She smiled, glancing at the Alfredo. "It looks amazing."

He looked up at her. "Everything looks pretty damn amazing."

They dug in, talking about their jobs and Julia between bites. They didn't talk too much about family or anything too serious. She knew that this was a decent first-date conversation and going into anything too serious would be hurtful. Maybe not for him, but definitely for her.

"So, we doing pretty good for our first date?" Ryan asked after they had been eating for a bit.

"I think so," she said, setting her fork and knife down. "It's been a while since I went on a first date. Or at least a good one."

"Really? So those other dates that you went on really sucked?"

She shook her head. "I've only been on two dates since Max, and they were okay. Nothing to write home about. I think this one's going much better. My first date with Max? That one sucked. I'm not going to lie. There was tuna fish involved, and a broken-down car. But it still ended pretty nicely."

She smiled, then froze, realizing exactly what she had been talking about.

"I'm sorry, Ryan. I didn't mean to bring him up."

Ryan reached out and gripped her hand, giving it a squeeze. But he didn't let go. "Max is part of your life. He's Julia's father, and you loved him. You were going to marry him. If you want to talk about Max the whole night, I'll listen. It's still a date, even if we talk about other people. He was part of your life. He's still a big part of it. So don't worry. I like to hear about him. You smile when you talk about him, and that makes me happy. Because if you didn't smile, if it hurt you too much, then I would know you weren't ready for this. So, talk away."

She wiped away a tear, giving him a watery smile. "Sometimes, Ryan, I think you're a little too good to be true."

"You say that, but you haven't seen me try to vacuum. I kind of suck at vacuuming. And dusting. Okay, I suck at cleaning."

She rolled her eyes, laughed, and continued their conversation. She only brought Max up a few more times, but she couldn't help it. Ryan just let her relax. And when she did, she talked about things that were important to her. Ryan was right, Max was still important to her. She would always love him. But she knew that she was moving on, or at least trying to.

She didn't feel bad about thinking about Max when she was with Ryan. Maybe others would have, but Ryan made it easy.

Ryan made a lot of things easy.

Maybe that should have worried her, and honestly, it did a little, but the food was nice, the conversation was much easier than she'd thought it would be, and Ryan made her smile.

There were those butterflies again, the ones that made her think. The ones that made her not exactly yearn but want something.

"So, Julia really tried to eat all the chocolate when you weren't looking?"

They were having their after-dinner coffees, something that she didn't normally do when she went out. But neither of them had wanted the night to end yet, and they were enjoying themselves. The place was busy, but it didn't look like the waiter was trying to push them out of their seats yet, so they stayed.

"Seriously, the first time she learned to crawl, she somehow got through the child-protection locks and tried to eat an entire bar of chocolate. My hidden stash. The one that I even tried to hide from myself because it was way too good—and a little too pricey."

Ryan laughed, his hand still on hers. Every once in a while, his thumb would brush along the flesh between her thumb and her pointer finger, and she'd hold back a shiver. She didn't even know if he was doing it on purpose. He was just touching her. As if he wanted to touch her.

She really, really liked it.

"Well, chocolate is the food of the gods. She's just learning early."

"I think too early. I don't even know when children are allowed to have chocolate. Well, I did, but all of those things just leave my mind when they're no longer important because I keep thinking of all the new things I need to know about kids."

"It's a little insane how many dos and don'ts and rules and regulations and everything it takes to have a kid these days."

"Well, children are hard."

"That's not what I meant. Even though we're not that old, I just feel like we're closer to the generation that threw their kids in the back of a pickup without seat belts than we are to the kids with all of the regulations. Not that I'm saying those are wrong. I kind of like the fact that I was forced to wear a helmet as a kid and always have a seat belt on. It kept me alive." He winced. "Sorry."

"It's fine, Ryan. It's amazing how many things we say on a day-to-day basis that have to do with death. I didn't realize it until I witnessed it firsthand. I lost Max, and I swear every single person at least once a day made a comment about how they were going to die if they didn't have this, or that something was killing them, or that their heart was beating so fast it could explode out of their chests, or they were going brain-dead. We just have those things in our vernacular. We don't mean them the way they sound. But when you're attuned to that, you can't help but notice it."

"I still don't want to hurt you by saying those words. I try to watch what I say and be aware that sometimes, using the vernacular as you put it, isn't being sensitive to others."

She shook her head. "I don't need you to be careful around me, Ryan. I hope you know that."

He looked at her then, his gaze boring into hers. She swallowed hard, not letting go of his hand. Her stomach once again filled with those butterflies.

The waiter came then, leaving the final check. They paid. Soon, Ryan would be taking her home, and the date would end.

But she didn't want it to end.

"I had a nice time tonight," she said later as he walked her to her door.

"Yeah? I didn't scare you away?"

She looked up at him then, her heart racing. "No. And maybe that surprised me. I tend to get scared easily."

He shook his head. "No. I don't think you do. I think you're much stronger than you think you are."

She let out a breath. "I hate that. Sorry."

He frowned. "What? The fact that I think you're strong?"

"No, just that phrase. I like the fact that you think I have strength, but it's the whole...*stronger than you think you are*. And it's not because it's not true, it's just the fact that everybody and their mother said that to me. Literally, and their mother."

"Really?"

They were standing on her porch, the wind a little bit too cold for them to be doing so, but she wasn't ready to go inside yet, and she didn't know if she was going to invite him in either. "Everybody always assumed that I thought myself weak. At least that's what the words sounded like to me when I thought about them. I know that's not what they meant. I know that they were trying to tell me that I was doing well, and that despite everything happening to me, that I was making strides. But it just made me think that they thought I wouldn't be able to handle it. And yet, I did. Because I had to. Because there was no other way to keep moving forward if I didn't handle it."

Ryan reached out and brushed his thumb across her cheek. "That's not what I meant. And I'm sorry I made you think about it that way."

"It's not you."

"It's me?" he finished for her, and she shook her head.

"No, that's not what I meant. People have a way of underestimating the power of their words. And I know they don't mean anything by it. I know when faced with loss and especially faced with other people's loss, they just don't have the words. And sometimes that's okay, to not have the words. I know it's on me that I'm feeling that way, but because I heard that phrase so much, sometimes, it just annoys me a little."

"Then I'll try not to say it again. Even if I do think you're pretty kickass."

She smiled then. "Really?"

"Very kickass. Abby?"

She swallowed hard again. "What?" Her voice was breathy.

"Can I kiss you now?"

"I want you to. But only if you come inside."

She hadn't meant to say that, but as soon as she said the words, she knew they were right.

He looked at her then, his gaze dark and intense. And then he nodded.

She led him inside, waiting for his kiss—and maybe more.

Chapter Six

Ryan could barely think straight and hadn't been able to since the moment Abby invited him into her place. His dick was hard, and his brain had gone on the fritz.

But he'd be damned if he walked away now.

To say that he wanted Abby was an understatement. He'd always wanted her. Had found her attractive from the beginning. Had loved the way she smiled and looked at him, making him freeze and wonder what to do next.

But this wasn't any of those times.

This was him. This was Abby.

And she had let him in. In more ways than one.

And now, all he wanted to do was lean forward and brush his lips along hers. But he needed to make sure that she was really okay with this. That she wasn't just acting in the heat of the moment and would regret it later.

He didn't want any regrets between them. He already had enough of those to last a lifetime.

"Are you sure, Abby?" He tucked her hair behind her ear and leaned forward. He didn't kiss her, but he wanted to.

From the heat in her eyes, the way her pupils dilated, he figured that she wanted him to as well. But he needed to hear the words. There would be no mistakes.

This would not be a mistake.

"I invited you in, didn't I?"

"I need to hear the words, Abby. I need to hear exactly what you want."

She smiled then, and he about swallowed his tongue.

"I want you to kiss me. And then I want you to help me strip out of these clothes, although these boots might take a little bit. And then I want you to stand there while I strip you out of yours. And then I want you to kiss me again, though maybe not on my mouth. I want you to make me feel. I want you to make me smile. I want you to make me come. I want it all. Is that okay? Do you think you can do that? Do you think you can take me right against this wall? Or maybe on the couch over there. Or maybe even in my bedroom?"

He swallowed hard, and then ran his thumb over her cheek, loving the way she shivered at his touch. She wasn't afraid of him. That much he knew. That much he could tell. And the fact that she could just come out and say those words right then? The fact that she could just tell him exactly what she wanted?

No wonder his dick was so fucking hard.

"I think that can be arranged. But you need to tell me what you want the whole time, okay? I don't mind being told what to do."

She laughed and then took a step forward, placing her hand on his chest. He wondered if she could hear the racing of his heartbeat. Because that was about all he could hear in his ears.

Thud. Thud. Thud.

A rapid succession of beats that made it hard for him to think.

Abby made it hard for him to think.

"Kiss me, Ryan. It's just you and me here. I promise."

He didn't know if that was quite true. They might be alone in this house, but they weren't the only two people there. And that was okay. Max would always be there. The fact that Michael was also on Ryan's mind made it a little harder, but he could just focus on Abby. She deserved that and more.

"I think that can be arranged." And then he lowered his head, gently brushing his lips along hers. She sucked in a breath, a barely audible sound, and it made him groan.

When she parted her lips ever so slightly, he let his tongue slide along hers, deepening the kiss. She moaned and wrapped her arms around his neck. That brought her breasts right to his chest, her hard nipples poking him even through her bra and dress and his shirt. He didn't mind; he wanted all of her. Wanted more of her.

And tonight, he was going to have her.

Tonight he would give her himself, as well.

"Where do you want me?" he asked, his lips practically still against hers. It was just a whisper, just a breath of words, but she had heard him.

"Anywhere. Anywhere." She repeated the word, her voice but a whisper. So he kissed her again, tasting her and teasing her ever so slightly.

She tasted of the wine from dinner, of the Alfredo they had shared between laughs. She smelled of tea, and he knew that was just the scent of her. She would always smell that way, of home and happiness. Every time he scented tea, he would likely get hard.

There was probably something wrong with him for that, but he didn't give a fuck.

He had Abby in his arms, and that was all that mattered.

"We'll go slow, I promise."

"What if I don't want slow?" she asked, her hand moving to his waistband. When she tugged, he smiled.

"Okay. The first time we can go slow. The second time? I can go as fast and hard as you want."

"Second time? Aren't you getting a little ahead of yourself?" She winked, and he leaned into her, his body inexplicably pulled to her. Hell, more than his body was drawn to her.

He grinned and then stole a kiss before cupping her face in both of his hands and kissing her even harder. Then he broke away to say more. "Let's just say I don't think I'm going to get enough of you just once. I hope you feel the same way."

"I think...I think that sounds about right."

And then they were kissing again, lost in each other. Ryan wanted more of Abby, wanted to taste every inch of her. And if she let him, he would do that tonight.

And maybe again tomorrow.

He probably shouldn't think about tomorrow. Probably shouldn't think about anything beyond right now.

Because if he weren't careful, he knew he could fall for her. And he couldn't do that. He didn't have enough of himself to give to her. It wouldn't be safe. Michael always ruined everything that Ryan touched, and he had to be careful.

And with Abby, he had to be even more gentle with her than with anyone else in his life.

She deserved everything from him—gentleness, calmness, *him*.

And he would do his best by her.

Even if that meant walking away after tonight.

"What's wrong? You went all still."

"I'm sorry. Forget about it."

She shook her head and took a step back, still touching him. "No, what's wrong?"

"I get lost in my thoughts sometimes, I can't help it. But I promise, I'm all here." And because he wanted to make that the truth, he pushed Michael, his future, and everything that might worry him out of his mind before he kissed her again.

"If you're sure," she whispered against his lips and then sank into him, her eyes closed as she kissed him back.

"I'm sure," he whispered.

He ran his hands through her hair, tugging slightly just to see how she liked it. When she groaned, he tugged a little harder and then wrapped her hair around his fist. He tipped her head back ever so slightly and then left her lips to trail kisses along her jaw, and then licked down her neck. When he left a single bite mark on the part where her neck met her shoulder, she shivered again in his hold, and he used his other hand to press at the small of her back, moving her even closer to him.

He knew she could feel the hard line of his erection against her stomach, and it made him even harder.

She didn't back away. If anything, she rocked against him even more.

She liked this, and damn, he liked it, too.

When she tugged on his pants again, he let go of her hair and slid his other hand down to her ass. And then he lifted, picking her up in his arms as if she weighed nothing. And she didn't really weigh much. She was perfect for his arms—perfect for him.

He shouldn't think about that.

Nothing was perfect.

He knew that more than most.

She wrapped her legs around his waist, and he kept his mouth on hers. He wanted to take her in the bedroom first.

Later, he would take her against a wall, or maybe against that couch.

But she deserved the bedroom for their first time.

She deserved soft sheets and even softer caresses.

Of course, she also seemed to like it when he tugged on her hair, so he would do that again. And do it often. And more than once. They got back to the bedroom, and he kept his mouth on hers before biting her chin.

She looked up at him, surprised, and then bit his chin in return.

"I like you with a beard. It's kind of hot."

"I like the beard, too. You like the scent?"

She licked his lips and kissed him hard. "Yeah. It's like honey this time."

"Yeah. I think there's lilac in it, too. Not quite sure. But I like the honey. Although it always makes me hungry."

"I'm sure we can find something for you to eat." She winked, and he laughed, not able to hold himself back.

He let her slide down to the floor, her feet touching softly. The way he did it, though, her whole body slid down his, each part touching.

If she hadn't known he was hard before, she was damn well sure of it now.

"I wonder what I could eat here?" He tapped his beard. "Do you have anything sweet?"

"Maybe. I guess we'll just have to see."

He kissed her again, and then slowly slid her dress up over her hips. His fingertips brushed along her skin as he did, over her tights. He swallowed hard as he licked down her neck, biting her again. When she raised her hands over her head, he pulled her dress over the curves of her body.

And then she was standing in front of him, in just a lacy black bra, tights, and her boots.

He had probably seen something hotter before, but he couldn't think of anything.

No. In fact, this might be the sexiest thing he'd ever seen in his life.

He was a damn lucky man.

And he wanted to keep her.

No, he wasn't going to think about that.

Just be in the now. In the moment.

He needed to make this all about her.

He slowly traced his fingers over the swells of her breasts, grinning as she sucked in a breath.

"Your curves are perfect." He cupped a breast with his hand. "See? Fits my hand perfectly."

"Good to know you have big hands."

He smiled. "It's not the only thing that's big."

She snorted and then reached between them, running her hand over his thick cock straining his jeans. He swallowed hard and rocked into her touch. Then he pulled away, shaking his head.

"You do that, and I'll come in my jeans like a teenager. Let me take care of you first."

"Take care of me?" she asked coyly.

He didn't have to explain. Instead, he went to his knees and kissed her through her tights. She sucked in a breath and ran her hands through his hair. And then he worked on her boots, knowing that with her tights on, he wouldn't be able to do what he wanted to do. Although, having her tights around her knees as he fucked her from behind might be fun. Later, though.

Right now, he wanted skin to skin.

Right now, he *needed* skin to skin.

He worked off her boots, and then while looking at her, he slowly rolled down her tights, taking her panties with them in one fluid movement.

Her eyes darkened even more as she looked down at him, running her hands through his hair as he looked up at her.

And then she reached around her back and undid the clasp of her bra.

When she tossed it away, her breasts fell heavily. Her nipples were hard, and Ryan knew they were aching.

It was all he could do not to stand up and put them in his mouth.

But her shaved pussy was right in front of him. He needed to touch her, needed to suck her. He needed everything.

"Ryan? What are you going to do now?"

In answer, he looked up at her and put one hand on her hip. With the other, he used this thumb to slowly trace her slit. She sucked in a gasp, and he grinned before using his thumb and forefinger to spread her ever so slightly in front of him. Her clit was already out of its hood, peeking, swollen, begging for his tongue. And so he leaned forward and licked her.

"Ryan." She called out his name, and he couldn't help move even closer and take more of her into his mouth.

She tasted just as sweet as he imagined, with a little tartness. Perfection.

He sucked on her clit and used his fingers to continue to spread her for him. He lapped at her, sucking, licking, kneading.

And then he used his other hand to slowly trace her lower lips before spearing her with two fingers.

She gasped again and almost fell back on the bed.

Luckily, he moved his hand from her to keep her steady, though he knew her knees were shaking.

His knees were shaking too, but thankfully, he was kneeling.

She put a hand on the edge of the bed and tangled the other in his hair, pulling his face closer to her.

He smiled as he licked and sucked at her. He fucked her with his fingers, loving her little moans and the way her breaths came in short pants.

And then when she came, arching into him, he kept his mouth on her, tasting every single drop of her orgasm. Before she could pull away, before she could tell him that she wanted him inside her—because that's exactly what she was going to say, because that's exactly what *he* wanted—he pushed at her slightly and then helped her sit on the edge of the bed.

"Ryan?" Her voice was a little groggy, and her eyes were fairly black with lust.

She looked beautiful when she came, and he wanted to see it again. So he put both of her legs on his shoulders and went back to eating her out. This time when she came, she fell back, her hands on her breasts as she panted his name. He licked up her second orgasm and then stood up so he hovered over her.

The fact that she was completely naked and he was fully clothed just made everything hotter. He didn't know why. But damn if he didn't want to just lean over and kiss her until she somehow came again by his touch alone.

That wasn't going to happen, though, not when he was already straining the seams of his jeans.

"I need you inside me."

He looked down at her and then licked her taste off his lips. "I had a feeling you were going to say that."

"I would throw a pillow at you, but I'm a little too weak to do it. So if you could just get a condom and get inside me, that would be great." She paused. "I bought a new box, just in case. They're in the drawer."

He leaned over her, her naked body pressed against his clothed one as he kissed her. He knew that she could taste herself on his tongue, and that made him even harder.

"I brought a condom, too. But the fact that you wanted to be safe for both of us? The fact that you thought that this could happen? It just makes me want to keep fucking you. Keep making love to you. Is that okay?"

She looked up at him, tracing her fingertips through his beard. When she gave him a slight nod, he swallowed hard. "I bought the new box for you. And for me. I wanted to be safe, and maybe I was putting the cart before the horse, but considering what we're doing right now, I'm glad I did it. And I'm glad you brought some. I'm glad you thought of our safety."

Maybe if they'd been younger, the idea that they were planning ahead would have been presumptuous, but not now. Having condoms on any date, just in case, was smart. It wasn't saying that you had to have sex, it meant that you wanted to be able to have sex if you wanted to. And that you weren't going to make a mistake by going bare on the first date. Accidental pregnancies and diseases were no joke, and he wasn't going to risk Abby or himself because they hadn't been thinking ahead.

He quickly went to the drawer she'd indicated and pulled one out. He had one in his pocket, but for some reason, he wanted to use hers. He'd gone damn insane. And then he pulled out a second condom and put it on the nightstand.

He winked at her. "Just in case."

"I think I said something about stripping you, but I think...I think I just want to watch you do it." Suddenly, she had one hand on her pussy, and the other on her breast as she watched him. The fact that she was getting herself off right in front of him?

Hottest. Thing. Ever.

He was very lucky he didn't come immediately.

He didn't think he'd ever stripped so fast. He almost choked himself with the buttons on his shirt, but that the idea she didn't laugh at him and instead continued to touch herself had to count as a win.

"You're so damn hot," he said as he rolled the condom over his dick.

"Same to you. Now, really, if you could just get in me. That would be great."

Ryan grinned and then crawled over her, leaving a soft kiss on each of her breasts, her neck, and then her lips on his way up her body.

"I've been thinking about this for probably longer than I should have," he said, honestly.

"Same." She searched his eyes, and he gave her a nod.

"Are you ready for me?"

"Yes. But, Ryan? It's been a while. So go slow."

He nodded again, having already guessed that. She might've gone on a couple of dates, but the way she had talked about them, he knew they hadn't gone well. He'd be the first person since Max. And that was why it wasn't just the two of them in the house. And he was okay with that.

He truly was.

He didn't want her to forget the person she had loved before.

But he also wanted to make this good for her, to make this just about them. At least for the few moments they had.

So he kissed her, placed himself at her entrance, and slowly slid into her. She tensed below him before melting. She was right, it had been a while for her. She was tight. Almost impossibly tight. But that was okay. He slowly worked his way in and out of her as he used one hand on her clit to make it easier for both of them. The other roamed her body before landing in her hair, helping to keep his mouth on hers as he kissed her.

They made love slowly, softly. Maybe they would go harder next time, and maybe there would be no next time. He hoped there was, but right then, nothing else mattered. It was just the two of them, only them. And so, when she came again, he caught her scream with his mouth. And then he came inside the condom deep inside her, pumping hot and hard. She was his, if only for the moment.

He wiped away the single tear that had fallen down her cheek, and he didn't feel bad about it.

He didn't know if he could.

"You're so beautiful," he whispered.

"You're not so bad yourself. Thank you for tonight," she

whispered.

He grinned.

"I probably shouldn't have said that while you're still inside me but thank you."

He kissed her again and then slowly slid out of her before taking care of the condom. He found a washrag in her bathroom, got it wet with warm water, and then went to clean her up. He kept his eyes on her, one hand holding hers, their fingers entangled as he wiped between her legs. They had used a condom, but he still wanted to make sure she was taken care of.

"You're pretty great, Ryan. Just saying."

He kissed her again. "And you're pretty great, too. Thank you for tonight," he whispered.

"I think we already said that."

"Maybe. But I think I've lost the ability to make my brain work and actually use words."

"I'll take that as a compliment." Then she sat up and swung her legs to the edge of the bed. That left him standing between her thighs, so he kissed her again.

"I have to text Adrienne soon and see if I'm going to pick up Julia or if she's going to drop her off. I know that's not the sexiest thing to say while we're both naked. But real life tends to get in the way of things like that."

He traced her jaw with his fingertip and nodded.

"I understand. Julia's number one. She should be. I'm going to kiss you again, and then I'm going to get dressed and leave. But, Abby? I hope you don't have any regrets. Tonight was...tonight was amazing, and not just what we did in this bedroom. And I'm going to see you at work, and hopefully, I'll see you again afterwards. So, tonight? Tonight was great. Tonight was you and me. I enjoyed myself. I hope you did too."

He hoped he was saying the right things because it wasn't easy trying to figure out what was the right thing to do and say when it came to the woman in front of him. She had a life of her own. She was a single mom. Julia would always come first, and Ryan would never be annoyed with that. But he also didn't want to move too fast or make promises that he couldn't keep.

His brother would likely make sure he wouldn't be able to keep those promises, after all.

Abby leaned forward and kissed his chest. "Thank you. And I'll see you at work. And, yes, I think I'd like to see you outside of it, too."

Then he kissed her again but didn't say another word.

He didn't want to ruin the moment with something stupid like asking her if she was really okay. Because after all, she would have to deal with her feelings regarding the fact that he had been the first person she'd been with since Max. He didn't know what to say about that and didn't want to encroach on her feelings. He would be there if she wanted to talk about it, even if it might be awkward.

He just really didn't want to make a mistake. He was good at those.

So he got dressed and watched as she did the same.

And then he kissed her before he left, wondering when he would get to see her again.

Wondering if this had all been a dream.

Because it had been perfect.

And nothing with him was ever perfect.

Chapter Seven

Abby knew the others knew *exactly* what had gone on during and after her date with Ryan the night before, and she hadn't even said a word. Apparently, it was written all over her face.

She'd had sex.

Dirty sex.

Emotional sex.

Damn good sex.

And her best friends knew.

Oh, they *knew*.

And now they were sitting in Thea's bakery, teas and coffees in their hands, staring at her with expectant looks on their faces. She would have to confess it all.

Because they might know, but they'd still want all the details.

It was how this whole friendship thing worked.

"So, are you going to tell us how your date went last night?" Adrienne asked, her eyes full of warmth as a smile tugged at her lips.

"Um." Abby knew she should have said something other than a word that wasn't really a word, but she didn't know how she was going to explain it.

She hadn't known what she was going to say, hadn't known how the date would go. It had been, well…she didn't want to say perfect because she, more than anyone, knew that nothing was perfect—except for her daughter—but it had been pretty darn close.

"Is that um a good um?" Thea asked, coming over with more pastries for them. They were in Thea's bakery, newly reopened since it had been closed for a little bit after the explosion that hurt Roxie's husband, Carter, and Thea herself.

Abby couldn't quite believe everything that had preceded those events or that her friends had actually been hurt.

But Roxie had said that Carter would recover nicely, and Thea was up and walking around. In fact, the other woman looked so happy and in love with Dimitri, the man that completed her in every way, that Abby figured that maybe she could put what had happened at the bakery behind them.

Of course, they'd probably be able to do that easier if Carter hadn't been hurt as badly as he had been.

So the bakery was open again minus the updated renovation that Abby knew Thea had wanted to do. They were also short an oven, but everything else was fine. The damage hadn't been as extensive as everyone thought in the beginning, and Abby was grateful for that. She had missed the bakery the few days it had been closed. She had missed her friends.

"It went great." She put her hands over her face and groaned. "Why am I making it sound like it was horrendous?"

"Why don't you tell me?" Kaylee asked, sipping her tea.

Kaylee was relatively new to their friendship circle. Newer than even Abby was. Kaylee was their Brushes with Lushes artist and coach. At least once a month, they went to Kaylee's art studio, drank some wine, and tried to learn how to paint. Everyone was much better than Abby was, although Roxie tended to be really hard on herself.

But Kaylee was their friend now, and Abby enjoyed opening up her circle just a little bit more to accommodate the woman. Something was going on with Kaylee, something that Abby didn't know the details of, but she had a feeling it had to do with Landon. Not that any of them were going to ask Kaylee, because the woman would probably just walk away after she gave them a look that shriveled them down to their bones. Kaylee was good at that, even though she was one of the sweetest people that Abby knew.

It didn't help that everybody's current focus was on Abby and Ryan, and not Kaylee and Landon. Well, Abby and Ryan as well as Roxie and Carter. But they weren't going to talk about that couple either.

Because Abby didn't know if there were answers for any of that.

"Abby?" Adrienne asked again, pulling Abby out of her tangled thoughts.

Yes, she was worried about her friends, but it wasn't like she could just up and ask them what was bothering them. If it was something as easy as a stubbed toe or just a bad day, she could ask, but there were so many other layers to these topics, and that made it complicated. She didn't have any right to dig into it or try to help. Because she, more than most, knew that forcing someone to talk about something that they weren't ready for only made things worse in the end. Her former friends up in Denver—not the Gallaghers or the Montgomerys—had tried to tell her that everything happened for a reason. That losing Max had a purpose in the end.

She hadn't wanted to speak to them again after that.

What purpose did losing the love of your life serve? What did Julia never getting to meet her father mean?

There hadn't been a purpose, only life. Only death.

And when the others started to drift away from her because they hadn't been able to deal with her grief, she let them.

Her friends here didn't pry. Oh, they were sticking their noses in right then when it had to do with Ryan, but they wouldn't pry unless she needed them to. And the fact that they were such good friends meant that they knew when to do it or not.

Right then, her meddling when it came to Roxie or Kaylee and how they were feeling, or why they were feeling it, was not appropriate.

Eventually, she would. At some point, she would try to help.

But for now, she knew they needed space.

She didn't. She was ready to talk.

"Okay, so the date was amazing." She knew there was warmth in her tone, even if there was also a little confusion.

The others clapped their hands, everyone looking happy, although Roxie and Kaylee looked slightly...off.

But they had both been quiet recently—too quiet.

Again, Abby would ask them if she could help when the time came. But now was not that time.

"And?" Thea asked, finally sitting down. Thea was constantly moving around, especially considering that she was still working, but she had also hired another staffer, who was doing really well for everyone and allowed Thea to have something called a life.

Abby couldn't wait for one of those of her own.

A life and help beyond the people she borrowed from Thea.

"And I had fun. We went out to dinner, we talked. We talked a lot."

"About what?" Adrienne asked.

"About Julia, work, and even Max." She winced, and Thea reached out and patted her hand.

"He was always going to come up, don't you think?" Thea asked, her voice gentle.

"I know. And Ryan didn't seem bothered by it at all. I don't think I talked about Max for all the hours we were together, but I did mention him a lot. But then again, you're right, he was a huge part of my life. He still is because of Julia. Even Ryan said as much. Of course, Max would probably still be a huge part of my life even if I didn't have Julia."

"I can't say that I know what you mean, but I understand. He was the love of your life." This time, Adrienne winced. "I don't know if I can say that, not anymore. I'm sorry."

Abby shook her head. "No, you're right. I always call Max the love of my life. And I don't know how I'm going to use the verbiage from now on after this. Because, yes, Max was the love of my life, and I will always love him. But I don't know what will happen if I fall for someone else." She quickly shook her head. "Not that I'm saying I'm actually going to fall for Ryan, but it's the idea that I was actually happy last night that makes it all mixed up in my head. And it's the idea that I have to come up with what I feel because I need the words, but I don't want to compare to what I had, even though I'm always going to try at first. That's how my brain works."

"You're so strong," Adrienne said and then shook her head. "Nope. Forget I said that. I know you hate when I say that."

Abby sat up a little straighter. "You do?"

"I noticed that you don't actually say anything but, yes, your eyes get narrower any time someone says that to you. I've been doing my best not to say it, but sometimes I just don't know what to say, and those are the words that pop out."

"I'm sorry. I think it's just a tic at this point."

"And it makes sense," Thea put in. "But why don't you tell us about the rest of the night? Because I heard from a reliable source that you didn't pick up Julia until much later than dinner would suggest."

Abby just grinned. "I have no idea what you mean."

"I saw your face, young lady," Adrienne said, trying her best to be prim and proper. But the piercings and the tattoos ruined the look a bit. "I saw the way you looked, and I saw how you purposely didn't look me in the eye because you didn't want to talk about it in front of Julia. And I let that pass. I've let a full morning pass, and yet we're here for girl time, and it's time for you to tell us what happened. And how much you liked it. And everything else. I mean, I can go in the back and get a baguette if you'd like to discuss measurements."

Abby threw her head back and laughed, the others joining in.

"You are not going into my kitchen to look for a baguette," Thea said, her voice stern. Although there was laughter dancing in her eyes, so Abby wasn't quite sure if Thea meant it. For all she knew, there was a baguette or something a little thicker that might join them at the table soon.

At that thought, Abby knew she was blushing, the heat of her cheeks warming her body.

"So?" Kaylee asked, her voice soft. "Should I ask how it was, or how you're feeling? Because I want to know both. We love you, Abby, and the fact that you're smiling like this? I think I love you a little more for it."

"And I think I could hug Ryan for it, too," Roxie put in.

Abby bit her lip and stirred her tea as she looked at her friends. "I didn't mean to sleep with him on the first date, but it just happened."

She was keeping her voice low, but they were at the special corner table where Thea knew that others couldn't really hear well. It's why she always sat them there. Abby didn't mind, and she knew that if any of the men came in for sweets, she would just pretend that she totally wasn't talking about having sex with Ryan.

She also knew that she couldn't stay here long and talk about it, because one of Thea's part-timers was working over at the tea shop, picking up hours that Abby could barely afford. They were testing it out, and Abby was doing her best to not think about it. But, hopefully, it would work out, and the new person could get some needed money while Abby got some needed help.

And if she kept thinking about work and money, maybe she wouldn't blush as hard when she thought about Ryan.

"Hello?" Adrienne said, waving her hand in front of Abby's face.

"We need the deets." Adrienne grinned, and Abby rolled her eyes.

"I'm not giving you details."

"Um, yes you are," Thea said, grinning. "We gave you details."

"And yet I'm a little worried that we know way too much about each other's sex lives."

"At least you have a sex life," Kaylee muttered and then looked over at everyone, her eyes wide. "Forget I said that. This isn't about me, this is all about you and Ryan."

"Oh, we're going to come back to that later," Adrienne said. "But we'll let you slide. Just for now. Because I know Abby needs to get back to the shop, and we need to know exactly what happened with Ryan. Every single little detail you want to share."

"You shouldn't have added the *you want to share* part," Roxie said, smiling for the first time. "Because now she's just going to tell you nothing."

"Fine, I'll tell you a little."

"Oh, don't say little when we're talking about sex with Ryan," Adrienne said, grinning.

"Fine."

"And don't say fine," Thea put in.

"If you would like me to continue, I'll actually tell you something. Or if you'd just like to keep cutting me off, I'll go have some tea in my shop." Abby smiled as she said it, and everybody rolled their eyes, leaning forward as if they were afraid she might whisper what she had to say.

Well, considering she was about to whisper it all, she didn't blame them.

"It was everything. I didn't know I was going to sleep with him until it was happening. And he was kind and sweet and sexy as hell. He didn't make me feel like I was doing anything too slow or fast or wrong. Not that I was doing anything wrong, but there was a moment there when I realized that, yes, this was my first time since Max, and while I wasn't comparing, I had that clutch. That little heart twinge that said, 'Okay, you can do this. You like Ryan. And you're not cheating.' And I wasn't. And he looked me right in the eyes, and I knew that he understood what I was feeling. I didn't know I could ever feel like that. I didn't think I could ever have that connection. And I know that there were no promises made, and I don't know what's going to happen next, but I don't regret it. Not even a little. Because he made me happy. He does make me happy. And even if we just remain friends after this and never go on another date, even if we never sleep with each other again, I know that he was exactly what I needed, and what I need right now. I don't really know what's going to happen next, but he made me happy. And I guess that's all that matters."

All four women were wiping tears from their eyes, and Abby didn't realize she had let a few tears fall herself until Roxie handed her a napkin.

"I'm glad that you're happy," Roxie whispered.

There was such longing there in that statement, so much yearning that Abby reached out and squeezed her friend's hand. Roxie met Abby's gaze and then pulled her hand away, obviously not quite ready to tell the world what was going on with her. Then again, Abby was just now getting used to telling the world about herself.

"So, he made you happy, but did he make you *happy*?" Adrienne emphasized the last word, and everyone giggled.

"Yes. Multiple times. If you must know, he's very good at what he does."

She lifted her chin, trying to look haughty. The rest of them just laughed.

"And on that note, I have to get back to my store, but I love you guys. Thank you for letting me talk to you about things that I didn't know I would ever be able to talk to anyone about. Thank you for just letting me be a dork. Because I don't know exactly how I feel, but I know that I'm okay feeling what I feel. And that's because of you guys, and because of Ryan. And on that note, I'm going to head out."

They all stood up, helping Thea clear off the table so she didn't have to do it on her own. Then they hugged and kissed before Roxie and Kaylee left to their cars, and Adrienne walked part of the way to Abby's store, stopping at her tattoo shop on the way so she could get back to work.

That left Abby alone at Teas'd when she sent Thea's part-time help back to the bakery. She reminded herself once again that everything would be okay.

She was sore in all the right places, warm in others. She didn't know if she would ever see Ryan again outside of work and maybe hanging out with the Montgomerys. Because although they had talked about it a bit, she didn't really know for sure.

Did she want to see him again?

If she thought about it, the answer was yes.

She did. But she didn't want to rely on that, didn't want to put too much pressure on Ryan. She knew he had secrets, knew he had scars that he didn't want to talk about. But then again, she was just getting used to talking about her own.

She didn't know if she wanted to fall in love again. She had been in love, and it had hurt so bad to lose it that she was only now clawing her way out of the abyss.

And though she knew in her mind that sleeping with someone and going on dates didn't automatically mean you were falling in love, Abby wasn't really good at casual dating. She hadn't even slept with Max on their first date, but she had with Ryan.

She wasn't the same person she had been before, wasn't even the same person she was two days ago at this point.

But she was trying to figure it out.

She didn't know what would happen next, and even though that worried her, it kind of thrilled her at the same time. She had so many schedules and lists when it came to her life and Julia, so many things that had to be done because she was a single mom and because she had lost Max.

But now she was trying to live in the moment, even if she wasn't really good at it.

She was learning.

One soft memory of Ryan at a time.

A few customers came in, and she helped them with their tea and their purchases, grateful that she would probably end up in the black for the month. She had been bringing in profits all year, and she did her best not to do a little dance in the middle of her shop and jinx it.

When the bell over the door rang again, she turned, smiling as Ryan walked in. She knew her smile was wide, and though she tried to rein it in so she didn't look like a dork, she knew it wasn't working.

She just looked at him and smiled even more.

There was definitely something wrong with her.

"You look nice," Ryan said, coming over to her. He didn't put his hands in his pockets this time, didn't stay away as if he didn't want to touch her. Or like he thought he couldn't.

Instead, he put one hand on her cheek and brushed his lips against hers. She closed her eyes, trying not to moan. He was so soft, and yet so hard.

And in this moment, he was hers.

She didn't mind that there might not be moments after this.

And if she kept telling herself, she'd be okay with it.

"You don't look too bad yourself," she said. "I say that often when it comes to you. I need to think of new lines."

"I like hearing what you have to say." He tucked her hair behind her ear. "I'm in between clients right now, but I thought I'd stop by and say hi. I know you were over at the bakery with the girls. I hope you had fun." He raised his brow, and she knew that he knew exactly what she and the ladies had talked about.

"I should feel embarrassed, but I have a feeling you know."

"Know that you and the girls were talking about our date last night? Yeah, I know, and I don't mind. The guys asked me about it, and I didn't go into detail, but I did say that we went on a date."

"I might have gone into a little bit more detail," she said, cringing.

Ryan laughed, that deep belly laugh that went straight to her core. "See? And now I'm going to have to look Adrienne in the eyes later today and know that she knows something that I'm not sure I want her to know."

"I'm sorry, Ryan."

"Don't be sorry. I'm just kidding with you. And I did come over here for a purpose."

"Peppermint tea?"

He shook his head, and her stomach filled with butterflies again. "I like the tea, but I think I like you more."

"You think?" Once again, her voice was a whisper. And not because she didn't want anyone to hear. Because it was just her and him, just them in the space.

"Oh, I know, but I didn't want to sound too forward."

"I don't mind, at least about that."

"Good, then let's do it again."

"The sex? Or when I talk about Max for hours?" She hadn't meant to blurt that out, but here she was, being a dork again.

"Either. Both? And you didn't talk about Max for hours. I just want to get to know you. I mean, I know you, but I want to know you more. And I want to go on another date."

"I think I'd like that."

Before they could say anything else, the bell over the door rang, and both of them turned.

When Ryan suddenly put his body between her and the person coming through the door, his shoulders going back, and his hands fisting at his sides, she knew that something was wrong.

And she knew that this might end badly.

"What are you doing here, Michael?"

Chapter Eight

Ryan's stomach lurched as Michael took another step into Teas'd.

Michael being here couldn't be good. In fact, Ryan knew that whatever Michael had in store, it would likely hurt everybody in the end. It always did when it came to Michael.

"What are you doing here, Michael?" Ryan asked again when his brother didn't say anything. Michael looked around the tea shop, and Ryan knew that his brother was taking in everything as if he were casing the place. Michael would see random bags of tea, containers for it, and teapots and handmade ceramics. He wouldn't see anything valuable, but that was his brother. He only saw value in monetary worth. Whatever he could use to get more drugs or use more people.

He wouldn't see the heart and the soul of the place. Wouldn't see all of the hard work that Abby had put into everything that she did. He wouldn't see the way she had arranged each of the areas so that people felt like they were at home and could just sit right down and have a cup of tea.

He wouldn't see the different flavorings and the ways that Abby did her best to make sure it felt like it was a new season with each one so her customers felt like they could just sip and enjoy their time.

Michael wouldn't see any of that.

He wouldn't see the value in what Abby had, or even in who she was.

But Ryan did.

And because he knew that Michael always saw what Ryan had, wanted what was Ryan's and coveted it for himself, Ryan had to get his brother out of this place before he screwed it all up. Ryan knew that he could screw up everything just fine on his own, he didn't need the help of his drug-addicted brother.

And Michael was completely stoned off his ass right then.

Ryan could see the glassy sheen in eyes so like his own set in his brother's sunken face. He could see the dark shadows beneath those eyes. He could see his brother's state in the way Michael suddenly twitched, itching a spot on his arm through his jacket. He could see it in the way Michael staggered just a little as he took another step into the store.

He could see it in the way his brother's eyes weren't completely tracking, even as he cased the place.

His brother was stoned. High off whatever he could get. Probably having used the last of whatever money he'd taken from someone else. Because Michael never got a job, no matter how many times his parents or Ryan had tried. Michael didn't like to work for his money. He liked it given to him. When they had been younger, their parents had obliged.

Ryan had gotten a job when he was a teenager, had wanted to earn his way because that was how he'd thought to outdo his brother. His parents' attention had been solely on Michael, and Ryan had wanted to be different. Had wanted *everything* to be different. He'd worked for his money rather than taking it all like Michael did.

His brother preferred just sitting down and letting other people take care of him.

But Ryan wouldn't let that happen.

He just didn't know how to get his brother out of this place.

"Nice place you have here," Michael said, his voice not slurred but very precise, as if he was doing his best to say every single word like he meant it rather than slurring.

"I'm going to ask you again, Michael. What are you doing here?"

Ryan felt Abby put her hand on his back. It should have strengthened him, should have sent some warmth through him like it usually did, but it did nothing. All it did was remind Ryan that Michael could screw up everything, even more than Ryan could do on his own. It reminded him that he needed to get his brother out of Abby's place and away from her life. *Ryan* needed to stay away from Abby. She deserved far more than a lover with a drug-addicted brother. She deserved far more than anything that Ryan could give her.

But he couldn't think about his need, couldn't focus on what he wanted and what he would be so sad to lose. He needed to focus on Michael.

Again.

"I can't just come and visit my dear brother? I mean, you don't call, you don't write. All you do is pretend that you know what the fuck you're doing. You know, I see you sitting here drinking tea like some fancy boy. Dad wouldn't have liked that. He never did like the fact that you like taking it up the ass, but then again, you usually enjoyed sticking it in a girl or a guy when you were done. It didn't really matter though, did it, Ryan? Daddy always liked you more than me. Maybe if I didn't mind taking it up the ass like you, he'd have loved me more."

Bile slid up Ryan's throat, and he took a step forward towards Michael, trying to get him out of the place before he did any more damage.

"Don't," he growled, but Michael ignored him.

Ryan knew that Abby was aware he was bisexual. It had come up in conversation in the past, and she hadn't seemed to mind. Between his friends, he was pretty sure that only one or two *weren't* bisexual. In fact, a trio of friends up in Denver even lived in a true triad. Sexuality didn't mean anything to them beyond the fact that it was their identity.

So the fact that Michael was saying things the way he was, probably trying to get a rise out of Ryan or embarrass him in front of Abby, wouldn't work the way Michael wanted it to.

Instead, all it did was put crude words into the air, though that might hurt his relationship with Abby.

Then again, that was probably what Michael wanted.

Because Michael never liked it when Ryan had anything of his own.

"You need to get out of here, Michael. Let's go and talk outside. Or get some coffee somewhere."

Not at Thea's.

Ryan's voice was firm, and far steadier than it had been when he was younger. This wasn't the first time Michael had come into a place where Ryan was, trying to screw everything up. And Ryan was afraid that it wouldn't be the last. But this *would* be the last time Michael ever stepped foot in Abby's place.

Abby was special. Abby was everything.

And he'd be damned if Michael hurt the woman Ryan cared about. The woman he wanted to be *his* woman. The woman who couldn't be his woman.

"You know, you keep trying to tell me what to do, and I don't think you understand, my brother. My twin. I don't think you understand that I don't have to listen to anything you fucking say. I didn't when we were younger, and I damn well sure don't now. All you had to do was help me, but instead, you sit on your high horse in your big fucking house and pretend that I'm not even your brother. I'm your flesh and blood, Ryan. I'm the one who means the most to you, at least I should."

Michael leaned over and looked around Ryan to wave at Abby.

"Hi there, doll. What's your name?"

"Don't talk to her."

"Oh?" There was a flash of triumph in his brother's eyes, and Ryan knew that he had made a mistake. He shouldn't have protected Abby, but then again, there was no damn way he wasn't going to protect her.

Michael was going to try and get what he wanted, and Ryan would do what he could to make sure that never happened.

"You shouldn't hide her," Michael said, looking at his brother. "I mean, she's a pretty little thing. Maybe we should share her like we did when we were younger."

Ryan took another step forward, and Michael took a step back, knocking into a display of tea canisters. They shook against the wall but didn't fall. That made Ryan freeze because there was no way he was going to destroy Abby's shop trying to get his brother out of the place. He would just remain calm and collected and make sure that Michael didn't fuck everything up.

Ryan lowered his voice and tempered his anger as much as possible. "We didn't share when we were younger, Michael. You'd need to be sober and not drugged off your ass to get it up." Ryan winced, annoyed with himself for letting his temper spill over. He shouldn't goad his brother, he just needed to get him out of there. If he did, everything would be okay.

Everything had to be okay.

Michael's eyes narrowed into slits. "You're an asshole. You know that? You think you're so high and mighty, and yet you're nothing. Just like you were when we were little."

Michael looked over at Abby again. "And I know what your name is, dear Abby." Michael giggled. *Fucking giggled.* "Oh, that's funny. Maybe I can write to you like all those little old ladies do. I wouldn't have those stupid fucking problems that don't mean anything, but you could help me with my dear brother. Do you know that he has a stick up his ass? I mean, he has all those tattoos, and he thinks he's so cool doing tattoos and piercings and living on the edge. But he's just some fucking hipster with too much money and time on his hands. Mommy and Daddy loved me more most of the time, and Ryan never liked that. So he made sure that I didn't get anything when they died. I mean, they kicked the fucking bucket, and I got nothing. There's something fucking wrong with that."

"I said don't talk to her," Ryan snapped. And how the hell did he know Abby's name? It wasn't on the shop, and she didn't wear a name tag. That meant that Michael had been watching them for more than just today.

That sent chills down Ryan's spine, and he shook his head, trying not to throw up. "You need to leave."

"Yes," Abby said, her voice firm and without a trace of fear in it. "This is my place of business, and you're not welcome here. You need to go before I call the police."

Michael just shook his head, still giggling. "You think you can tell me what to do? A bitch thinking she can tell me what to do? You know nothing, just like you, Ryan. Little fucking Jon Snow who knows nothing but is apparently good with his tongue. Because the only way you can get her is by using that mouth of yours. I bet that beard feels good between your thighs, doesn't it, little bitch?"

Ryan took a step forward and grabbed his brother by his leather jacket. "I need you to fucking leave."

"I don't think so." Then Michael wiggled away, smashing his elbow into Ryan's gut.

Ryan hadn't been expecting that, and sucked in a breath as he tried to grab his brother.

But Michael ducked and threw out his hands, knocking over a display of teapots before he did it again to a shelf of canisters.

"What the fuck are you doing? Get out of here. Stop it." Ryan shouted the words and tackled his brother to the floor, knocking over another set of teapots in the process.

He had his brother on the floor but looked over at Abby, who had her phone to her ear, probably talking with the police. She was pale and not saying a word to him, just telling whoever was on the other end to come over. The fight must have been loud—though Ryan couldn't hear anything over the pounding of the blood in his ears—because the Montgomerys were soon over at the store, ready to help out.

Mace had Adrienne behind him even as she tried to push through, probably trying to see what the fuck was going on just like the rest of them.

"Mace, let me in. I need to make sure Abby's okay."

Landon pushed his way through, his shirt off even in the cold, new ink on his shoulder. Ryan had forgotten that Mace was working on Landon's tattoo today, meaning the whole merry bunch was there, even Dimitri and Thea, who apparently had been at the bakery. As each person looked at Michael, they paused, glancing between Ryan and his twin.

It wasn't every day that his friends saw a distorted mirror image of someone they knew.

Everyone was front and center to see his fucking drug-addicted brother lying on the ground, everything torn, shattered, and broken around them.

And Abby looking at Ryan as if she had seen a ghost.

Or maybe as if he were beneath her.

And that would be true.

Because without Ryan being there, Michael probably wouldn't have come into the shop at all.

If Ryan had been faster or smarter, he would have gotten Michael out of there before he destroyed anything. Instead, all Abby's newest and most expensive displays were ruined, and it was his damn fault.

"The cops on their way?" Ryan asked as Mace and Landon and Dimitri all circled him. Thea and Adrienne went over to Abby, holding her close and whispering to her. They were probably making sure that she was all right and telling her that everything would be okay.

And it was going to be okay.

As long as he had nothing to do with her. As long as he walked away and made sure that she would always be fine, that this would never happen again, she would be okay.

"I called the police," Abby said, her voice wooden. "They're on their way. If you would just keep him here…"

"What the fuck is going on?" Mace asked, anger in his voice.

"Meet my brother, Michael."

"You're going to pay for this. No one fucks with me." Michael shook under Ryan's hold, and the other guys in the room came closer, ready to help.

"Shut up." Ryan put his hand on the back of Michael's head and pushed it to the floor. Maybe he would have tried to be a better brother and not hurt Michael, but he was so fucking tired. *So* fucking tired of all of this.

Why couldn't his brother just leave him alone? The more Ryan had helped in the past, the worse Michael got. So Ryan had stopped. He had pushed his brother away, just hoping that Michael would be able to find peace.

Ryan had never looked for his own. He had thrown himself into his work and tried not to make others care about what was wrong with him or worry about what he needed. Then he made a mistake. A big fucking error when it came to Abby.

He deserved anything he got.

But Abby didn't.

"Well, damn," Dimitri said, his voice low. The guys knew about his brother, at least some of the details. It was hard to have drinks and wings twice a week for over a year and not share at least some things about yourself.

They had wanted to know about Ryan's life, and he had mentioned Michael. And that meant the guys' women probably knew about Michael, too.

"I'm sorry," he said, looking at Abby. She just gave him a tight nod, and he knew that this was the beginning of the end. He'd fucked up. Then again, that's what his family did.

"Let me help clean up," Adrienne said and then stopped herself midstride. "No, I guess the police need to see this, don't they? Ryan, do you have him? Should the guys be helping you?"

"We've got it," Mace growled, and soon, all four men were helping keep Michael down, their eyes on the women in the room since the aggression in the air intensified with each passing moment. It only calmed slightly when the police arrived.

All of them talked with the cops and gave statements as the authorities pulled Michael out of the way, taking in the scene and doing their job. Ryan had a feeling that this wouldn't be the end of it. Jail time, and a little slap on the wrist for destruction of property and threatening wasn't going to stop Michael. It never did.

Ryan couldn't look at Abby. He was afraid that if he did, he'd see the disgust in her expression, the hurt.

He was so fucking embarrassed. *So* fucking ashamed.

It was one thing to say that, yes, he had a brother who was a drug addict, it was another when he showed up in your life and screwed everything up. It was yet another thing when he was suddenly there in your face, screaming and saying crude things that no one should ever say or have to hear. It was still more when that person came in and destroyed the things that you loved.

Ryan knew that Abby was doing well in her shop, but it was still early enough that he was afraid that if insurance didn't cover what had happened, she would lose everything. Well, he wasn't going to allow that to happen. At least he would do his best to never let that happen.

As the police took Michael close to the door, his brother looked Ryan in the eye. "You're a fucking betrayer. Look what you did to me. Look what you left me with. You think you deserve this life? You're nothing. One wrong move, and you're right beside me. Needle or not."

The police pulled Michael out of the building, out of everything that Abby had worked so hard for. And Ryan just stood there, his fists at his sides, a small cut on his hand from one of the teapots that had shattered on the floor. He didn't know when he'd gotten cut, but it had probably happened when he knocked Michael down.

The cut shed a single droplet of blood on Abby's floor, and he noticed the way the others looked down at it—most likely looked down on *him*.

"Okay, let me help you clean up now, they took photos," Adrienne said, her voice soft.

"Let's just leave it for now, close up for the night. Maybe go get some coffee?" Abby's voice started to break, and everyone looked at Ryan as if it was his job to go over and hold her. As much as he wanted to do that, that wasn't him anymore. He couldn't hold her. He didn't have the right.

He knew he had been falling for her already—falling for her smile, for everything about her. And he knew that if he stayed, he'd hurt her even more than just this night had.

So he glanced at her, looked at the wideness of her eyes, the paleness of her face. It would be forever etched on his mind. And then he looked at the door. "I'll help clean up tomorrow. But I can't do this. I need to go. I'm done."

Nobody said a word, but Abby moved forward. She put a hand on his arm, but he didn't look down at her. As much as he wanted to, he didn't turn her way. Because if he did, he'd break down, and he'd want to stay. And if he stayed, he'd hurt her.

"I've got to go. I'll pay for it. But I've got to go."

He paused. "I'm sorry." He let out a breath. "But I'm done."

And then he walked out, leaving a mess behind him like he always did when it came to his brother.

Maybe Michael was right, maybe Ryan wasn't so different, after all.

Ryan would help clean it up, and then he'd walk away. Find a new life...a new something. Because he couldn't stay. He couldn't even look at Abby.

Because he'd break.

Break more than he already was.

Chapter Nine

Abby watched Ryan walk out of Teas'd and wondered how she'd been so slow as to let that happen without saying anything. Honestly, she'd been so stunned by it all that she was still in a state of shock and was two steps behind when it came to her reactions.

She'd let Ryan walk away.

How could she have let him walk away?

Adrienne hugged her close, and Abby leaned into her friend, needing them all more than she thought possible. Yes, she was trying to lean on others more, but right then? She desperately needed it, even knowing that she wasn't going to do it for long because she needed to go kick some ass.

"Thea? Can I borrow your car?" Abby would be getting her car back the next day, but she still had to rely on others to get anywhere. While she was grateful for the help, she needed her own vehicle.

Thea reached into her pocket and handed over her keys without a word, but Dimitri put his hand on hers and handed his keys over instead.

"Take mine. Thea will need the bakery keys on hers," he reminded them all. "And go kick his ass, Abby. We all need an ass-kicking every once in a while."

"Don't remind me," Mace muttered, and the women nodded.

Landon came toward Abby, and she tried not to notice that he was still shirtless. It had already been a weird day. "You're good for him, Abby. He just needs to realize that. Kick his ass but make him talk. If he talks, you can get through to him."

Abby went up on her toes and kissed Landon's cheek. "I will. And I could say the same about you."

Landon narrowed his eyes. "One emotionally damaged man at a

time, thank you."

She rolled her eyes, knowing he wasn't exactly kidding, but she didn't have time to worry about him just then. The Montgomerys and others would take care of Landon and make sure his tattoo was finished as well as, you know, get him a shirt. The little things first.

She, on the other hand, had to deal with the man who'd just walked out on her because he was scared. Don't get her wrong, she'd been scared as well, but she wasn't about to let Ryan go. Not like this.

Not when she'd taken a chance.

She wouldn't allow either of them to mess this up because they were scared. She'd already gone through enough in her life. She couldn't let that happen.

Abby quickly said her goodbyes and headed to Dimitri's car, thankful that her friends were already planning to let her borrow it. Abby didn't know if she would have asked before everything that happened recently. She'd been so sure of herself, so used to doing everything on her own. She might have missed out on a lot.

But that didn't matter now. The only thing that did was Ryan. And he wasn't in the parking lot. He wasn't anywhere near.

She didn't think he would go to a bar, not after what had just happened with Michael, and she didn't believe that he'd go to the jail to bail his brother out either.

No, he would go home. To his big, empty house where he could be all alone and stew in his own misery.

Well, fuck that.

Abby wasn't going to let that happen.

The roads were a little slick but not too bad, and she was grateful that Dimitri's car was great with the weather. She pulled into Ryan's driveway, right next to his car, and let out a breath. She'd been right. He was home.

She didn't want to say that he was going to pay for leaving her like that, but it would be pretty damn close. Anger surged through her veins. She wasn't mad at Ryan, she was angry that he'd given up. But his life had been dealt another blow, and he had turned around and done the same to her.

Well, that just wouldn't stand.

She slammed the car door and made her way to Ryan's front door. She rang the doorbell, once, twice, then three times, her hands shaking as she did.

Maybe the adrenaline from what had happened at the store was finally wearing off and she was starting to freak out. Well, she could do that later. First, she needed to make sure that Ryan understood exactly what was going on.

Because there was no way she'd let it end like this.

It was going to end on her terms or his. Their terms.

Not Michael's.

She was about to ring the doorbell again when Ryan opened the door, his eyes wide, a closed beer bottle in his hand, and his shirt unbuttoned.

It was very hard to concentrate on being angry with him and the entire situation when all she could do was stare at his chest.

His very sexy chest.

A chest with the perfect amount of hair that made her want to growl, and ink everywhere there wasn't hair.

She really, really wanted to touch that chest.

But first, she needed to let her anger out.

"Can I come in?" she asked as she pushed her way into the house.

She wasn't usually this forward. In fact, she was usually only this way with her business. Except for when she had been in bed with Ryan. Then, she had been just as forward as he was. And it had been fun. Good. Neither of them fighting for control but pushing each other to go further. To fly over the edge as they came.

That had been fun.

But her standing up for herself like this? She wasn't really good at it.

But she'd be damned if she let what had happened earlier change and ruin everything.

Ryan closed the door behind her and then turned around on his heel. "I guess you can just come in."

"Thanks. We need to talk."

He pinched the bridge of his nose and let out a breath. "I don't want to hurt you, Abby, but you need to go."

She ignored the little clutch in her belly at his words. She would let him off the hook this time and not get too angry. She wouldn't lash out at him for pushing her away. She understood the desire, the need. She had done enough of that when she lost Max. But she wasn't about to walk away just then.

"No."

"What?"

"Hell no, actually. I'm not leaving. We're going to talk. Because that's not how we do things. We don't just run away when things get hard. You helped me when I needed you, and I'm trying to help you now. So let me do it."

"This isn't the same as helping you out of a snowbank. This isn't the same as a car accident on an icy road. Everything about this is far worse than just icy roads."

"Then tell me what this *is*."

"You saw what it is. You saw what my brother did. I don't want you in the middle of that. I don't want that to touch you. You deserve so much more than that."

"I'm going to stop you right there, Ryan. Because no one gets to tell me what I deserve other than me."

He looked a little sheepish and set the closed beer bottle down on the hutch near the entryway. "I don't want to hurt you, Abby."

"You keep saying that, but that doesn't make it completely true."

"But it *is* true."

"No, it isn't. Because you pushing me away like this is going to hurt me. It's not hurting right now because I think I'm still in a bit of shock over everything that just happened and I'm not feeling much pain. But I'm going to feel pain if you just push me away and ignore me like this. I want to help you, Ryan. I want to know exactly what happened and why. I don't blame you. I can't blame you. But you have to tell me. Because that person? Your brother? He wasn't you. Everything he said today meant nothing. All he did was show me what kind of ass he is. He didn't do anything to show what kind of man you are. Because I know what kind of man you are. And that man is nothing like your brother."

Ryan took a step forward, brushing his finger along her jawline. "It's not as simple as that."

"Then tell me." She swallowed hard. "Tell me."

"My brother's a drug addict."

She nodded. "I know. And I'm sorry."

He shook his head. "I was sorry for a long time, and then I couldn't be anymore."

"Then start at the beginning. I know this thing between us is new, but we were friends before everything changed. Let me be your friend.

Let me be here. Don't walk away, Ryan. Don't walk away from this when it's just beginning."

Ryan looked at her for so long, she was afraid that he would say no. She worried that he would tell her to leave and that he never wanted to see her again. He'd already tried to do that earlier, and she'd forced him to look at it another way. She hoped that she hadn't made a mistake.

"Come with me into the living room. Sit down while I pace or something. I just...I don't know what to do."

"Then just talk. And I'll listen."

She followed him into the living room, looking around his large house as she went and wanting to see all of it. Maybe that time would come. Perhaps he wouldn't push her out of his life fully, and she'd be able to see everything.

"My brother has always been selfish. And maybe that makes me a little selfish for thinking that, but I couldn't help it growing up. No matter what I did, I was never good enough. He might have said that I was the favorite, but that was never really the case. My parents loved my brother. He's my twin, you know."

She nodded. "I know." Michael had mentioned it, but she couldn't have missed the resemblance anyway. Even with the drugs on Michael and life that had been leeched from him.

"I'm an Air Force brat, meaning I moved around a lot as a kid. That's why I am decently good at driving in the snow here because it's not as bad as the snow was in northern Japan."

Her eyes widened. "You used to live in northern Japan?"

He nodded. "Yeah, at the end of high school. Snow there sucked. But that's where I learned how to drive. And then I had to learn how to drive on the right side of the road. But that doesn't really matter."

"Everything matters. All the little parts that make us who we are...all those things matter."

"Maybe you're right. But I'm taking a long time to figure out what I want to say."

"I'm here." She leaned forward as he paced around the living room. She wanted to walk with him, wanted to touch him. Wanted to do anything to make this easier for him.

But she knew as soon as she did that, she would pop the bubble, and maybe things would change. Maybe he would walk away, and she wouldn't be able to get anything out of him.

So she sat where she was, and she waited.

"We moved around a lot, and because of that, I only had my brother. It's hard to make new friends when you're constantly moving from place to place. I got good at being sociable when I needed to be, giving a little bit of myself as I walked around and met new people. I was good at fitting in with any situation, even if I didn't give myself completely. I never really wanted to because I knew we would be moving again, and then I would just have to start all over. Michael really wasn't the same way. He threw himself into friendships and relationships, at least he used to. Especially when we were kids. But then we'd be ripped from it, and he'd cling to me. And when I wasn't enough, and he couldn't figure out how to form relationships with other people, he flung himself into other things. He needed that adrenaline rush of having a best friend, of having attention focused on him. He went to drinking first. Because that made him popular. Even in middle school."

She pressed her lips together, understanding. "When we finally figured out who we were as individuals rather than just twins, we also had to deal with the fact that we were constantly moving. That the connections that we had were constantly fraying at the edges. And so, my brother then threw himself into drugs. He was in high school the first time he OD'd. And he did it because he wanted Mom and Dad to pay attention to him. Our parents had some money, and it wasn't from the military. Hell, the military pays shit…but you know that."

She nodded.

"So, my parents put Michael into a good rehab center, and they ignored the situation. They ignored the whys of it. They were both military, you see. Sometimes, one would be off for six months at a time, sometimes nine months on remote. TDYs are ridiculous, but it was what they did. They fought for our country, and I was damn proud of it."

"That's good."

"They didn't die because they were in the military. But when they did finally pass away, I think part of Michael broke. My parents gave Michael everything they possibly could to make him better. And Michael couldn't do it. There was just something about him that made him throw himself into every situation, to the point where drugs were his only answer. And he used people, broke people, and did everything that he could to make sure that he got what he wanted. And when he didn't, he broke even more."

Ryan let out a breath, and Abby just listened. "I didn't want my brother to die, but sometimes I think it would be easier if he did. And that makes me a horrible person, but he got me put in jail once because he stole my identity. We're twins. Apparently, it's easier than you think. He got me in bar fights, got me in trouble with my exes. He would pretend to be me and do so much shit that it was ridiculous. He doesn't look anything like me now; the drugs and the alcohol hurt him and aged him at least twenty years. But it's hard to love my brother. When I try to take care of him, it only enables him. A couple of years ago, I took a step back and told myself I wasn't going to do that anymore. I'd lost my parents and I was losing my brother, but I couldn't lose myself. And, yeah, maybe that's selfish, but fuck it. Every time I helped, he just went further and further over the edge. I just knew he was going to die no matter what I did. I took a step back and told myself I wasn't going to enable him anymore."

"That's good." She didn't know what else to say, not yet.

"Maybe, but he still blames me. Blames me for so much shit. He shows up every once in a while, no matter where I move, and tries to take my money, my house. Tries to take my friends." He looked her right in the eyes. "Tries to take those I care about."

"Okay. He's not going to."

"This is just the start."

"No, you tried to end it before, and we're going to make sure it's ended. Because you're not alone this time. And I'm not just talking about me. You know that Thea, Adrienne, Dimitri, Shep, Shea, Mace, Landon, and even Kaylee will all be there for you. Roxie and Carter will be there for you. I'm going to be there for you."

"I don't want them to get hurt." Ryan stuffed his hands into his pockets, and she shook her head, standing up so she could move around the coffee table and be right next to him. She put her hand on his chest, soaking in the warmth of his skin and feeling the heartbeat beneath her palm.

"He's not you. You can't put what he does on you. You can't put every single decision he's ever made on yourself. You were a military kid, too. You had to learn how to deal with new situations and new people. And you didn't turn into a drug addict."

"Abby."

"No, it's my turn. You didn't fall into the abyss like him. And am I sad that he's there? Yes. Because it hurts you. But he made his own decisions. And, yes, you've tried to help him. Your parents tried to help him. It wasn't enough. At least that's what he thought. But you did everything you could. And if you want to continue to help him, then go for it. But if you want to try and protect yourself for the first time? Then do that. Because addiction is a disease, but at some point, the people around the addict have to take care of themselves as well."

"He could have hurt you today." There was such a growl in his voice that Abby knew that this was one of the biggest parts of why he'd tried to push her away.

"No. Because you were there."

"But he knew your name. That means he was watching you before."

She held back a shiver and nodded. "And now the cops have him. And I'm going to press charges. And maybe they'll keep him locked away. But you were there, and I knew I wasn't going to get hurt. Am I sad about what happened in my shop today? Yes. Am I going to miss some money that I would have made from that stuff? Yes, but I have insurance. And it's just things. Believe me. With everything else going on. It's just things."

"I don't want you to get hurt."

"Then don't hurt me. Don't put what your brother's done on yourself. Just know that you're not alone. I'm here. And I don't want you to walk away. Don't push me away, Ryan. Please."

She was so afraid that he would tell her to go, to calmly say that it was over between them.

She didn't want it to be over. She wanted to know Ryan better. Wanted him in her life. This was so new, just the cusp of what it could be. But she was taking a chance on herself, taking a chance on them, and she desperately wished he would take a chance as well.

And when he didn't answer, she felt like the world was falling away beneath her, her stomach lurched, and her heart raced.

But he didn't say anything.

Instead, he lowered his head and brushed his lips along hers. A gentle kiss, a sweet caress.

Everything would be okay.

Everything had to be okay.

Chapter Ten

"I'm sorry." Ryan lowered his head and rested his forehead on hers. "I'm sorry for reacting like I did. For pushing you away. For doing everything that I did like that. I just reacted. And it was stupid. But I'm sorry."

"You don't get to be sorry." She paused. "Because you don't have to be. I lost someone before. And I thought I lost it all. I thought everything was over. But it wasn't."

Ryan ran his hands through her hair and looked down at her. "I don't know how you do it."

"What? Live? It's the only thing I know how to do anymore."

He pulled her into his arms, holding her close. She was so damn strong, but he knew she hated those words, so he wasn't going to say them. But she was. He'd walked away because he needed time to think, and was so afraid that she was going to get hurt because of him. So he'd taken away her choice in the matter, and he regretted it. But now she was here, and he'd have to figure out what to do next.

"I don't know what I'm going to do about Michael, but I don't want to lose you because of it."

"Then don't let Michael matter when it comes to you and me. He's going to be a part of this because he threw himself into the situation, but that doesn't mean you have to let him be the main part. I don't know what's to come with his charges or anything that has to do with him and his future, but it doesn't have to be *your* future."

"He always has a way of making it feel it had to be."

"Then don't let it. And I know that seems basic, but it was the only way I could move on when I needed to." She pulled away, letting out a breath. "When Max died, I tried to make sure I could figure out how to move on, how to be who I was, learn what I needed to be. But it wasn't always easy. It isn't supposed to be. I was pregnant when Max died. We'd just found out the sex of the baby, and we had put off our wedding because we wanted to hold her together while we said our vows."

Abby shook her head, a small smile on her face.

"It seems silly now, wanting to hold an infant that would probably cry and poop and not really enjoy itself while we were saying our vows, but that's what we wanted. We were starting a new life, cancer or not. But the cancer came back, and it came back hard."

Abby looked Ryan right in the eyes, and he swallowed hard, knowing that she didn't talk about Max like this often. He was going to listen, and he would treasure it for what it was.

Trust.

She was trusting him with this part of herself, and he was going to do his best not to take that for granted.

"I thought my life was over when I lost Max. But it wasn't. The cancer that he had when he was a kid came back more than once. But it came back the hardest that last time. It wasn't one of those cancers that you see a ribbon for, or one of those that you can buy a can of soda and think you are donating when you really aren't and can think everything is fine. Because you know that nothing is fine when it comes to cancer. They call it the Big C and make all these slogans and say that everything will be fine if we can just find a cure. But they can't. Not yet. There's so much wrong with the world, but the fact that we can't figure out how to save someone in the prime of their life? Sometimes, I feel like that's one of the worst."

She shook her head, and Ryan stayed silent, reaching out for her when she came close in her pacing. She didn't move away from his touch, and for that he was grateful.

"Max met a friend when he was in treatment. Someone that he knew from back in his first treatment days. That's how I met the Montgomerys. Murphy Gallagher had cancer, and he lived. One of the nurses at the outpatient center was actually marrying into the Gallaghers, so she dealt with Max more than Murphy because of the conflict of interest and all that. But anyway, the Gallaghers had already married into the Montgomerys up in Denver, and then I met all of the Montgomerys after Max's death. And if you think the Montgomerys here in Colorado Springs are large, they're even bigger up in Denver."

He nodded, his eyes still on hers. "I know a few of them, so I get it." His lips quirked into a smile but he knew it didn't reach his eyes.

Between talking about drugs and death, it was kind of hard.

"Max was supposed to be fine. The cancer was going away, and the treatments were working. It just took such a toll on his body. He was so tired all the time, but he always laughed. I loved his laugh. It was just this big belly laugh that made you smile. And even if I didn't find whatever he was laughing about funny, I always joined in because of that laugh. And so, when we knew that the treatments were going better, even if they were taking more of a toll on him than usual, we planned to get married. We were going to have our Julia, and we intended to invite the Gallaghers and the Montgomerys to our wedding. They were probably going to outnumber Max's family, and since I didn't have any family of my own, they were really going to sprinkle into both sides of the aisle. But it was fine. We were making our own family. We were making our own future."

She wiped a tear from her face and looked up at him. "Max had a blood clot. A one in one hundred chance when it came to the drug that was supposed to save his life. That blood clot moved through his heart right in front of me. He looked right at me, his eyes wide, and I knew. He knew. He *knew*." She repeated. "I loved Max with everything I had. And he died right in front of me. I know they say that he probably didn't feel much pain, but I heard the sound of his voice when he died. I saw the way his body went tight. How his skin turned ashen. I saw the way he clutched at his chest. I know he died quickly, but there was pain. And I saw it all. They were really afraid that I was going to lose the baby right then because I fell to my knees, screaming."

She let out a breath.

"People helped me. I don't remember who they were. I just remember looking at Max and knowing he was gone. That he wasn't going to raise Julia, that he wasn't going to be the dad that I wanted him to be. He wasn't going to be with me at the altar saying our vows as we dealt with an infant. There wasn't going to be anything more."

"Abby, you don't have to continue."

"No, the hard part's over. Well, at least that hard part. Because Max was gone, and we weren't married, and even though he had filled out a lot of paperwork to make sure that I was the power of attorney, there were a lot of other things that I couldn't do since I wasn't legally his wife. But none of that matters anymore. In the end, I had the little bit of money that we had saved for each other, and I moved down here to try and start a new life. Because you know what the hard part of having those around you fall is?"

He shook his head, wanting to hold her but knowing that she needed to be strong right then.

"The hard part is living. Because that person's gone. They're not coming back. And you have to live. You have to go through the motions, through the paperwork, through the next day and the next. You have to remember to drink water. You have to remember to take a breath. And I had to remember to do that for two. I was alone in the room with nurses and doctors when Julia was born, but that was because I wanted it to be just me and Julia. I knew Max was in the room with me, even if he wasn't there physically. But I wasn't alone, not fully. The Gallaghers were in the waiting room. And then the Gallaghers and the Montgomerys helped me move down here. Oh, I tried to push them away. I tried to do things on my own because that's what I thought I needed to do. It isn't until just recently that I realized that I really can't do everything myself. But I'm learning to ask for help. Because I'm living. I've gone through grief. I'm still going through it day by day. But I'm okay, Ryan. Because I had to be. Because I want to be. And I'm telling you all this not so you can cry with me or feel sorry for me. I'm telling you this because I know you're grieving, too. You're losing Michael a little more each day, and yet it isn't like with Max when he was gone in that instant. You lose Michael every time he comes back into your life. And I know it's hard, but you're living. You have a job, you have this house." She paused. "You have me. If you want. Because you have me. Because you're not losing me. Okay? You don't have to lose me."

Ryan looked down at her steady hands. Steady. Not shaking. She was so damn strong. "I'm not going to tell you that it's a different kind of grief because you understand that. You, more than anyone, know that. But I don't want to lose you, Abby. I never wanted to lose you. I was just afraid that if I had you, Michael would ruin it."

She took a step forward, putting her hand on his chest again. He loved it when she touched him, loved everything about it. "Then don't lose me."

And so he kissed her again, knowing that she had taken a huge step for him, and all he had to do was take that step with her.

He kissed her more, holding her close as she leaned into him. "I want you in my life, Abby. I want every part of you." He knew they were just starting, that they had so much more to give, so much to learn about each other, but this was the first step.

He wanted more with her, but he knew that they would figure it out.

Together.

"Then take me," she whispered.

So he did.

First by slowly stripping her out of her clothes, then doing the same with his own. He lowered them to the soft rug he had in the living room, gently licking at her skin. She arched for him when he cupped her breasts, then panted when he touched her between her thighs.

They made love on his rug, surrounded by a roaring fire with snow falling outside. He plunged into her after getting the condom from her purse, each of them sucking in a breath as they both fought not to come immediately.

She bit his jaw, and he rocked into her, wanting to go slow but knowing that it wasn't easy when it came to Abby.

She licked his neck, and he thrust again.

Then she slid her hand between them, cupping him at his base before sliding him over her wetness.

And then he moved faster, harder, and they both came, panting each other's names even as they continued to move, clinging to one another as if they only had each other, like there were no worries in the world.

Tomorrow the world would change, and they would have to figure out what to do with Michael, Julia, Teas'd, and the rest of their long list of worries, but for now, they just held each other, petting one another as they fought to catch their breath.

And for now, that was what Ryan needed. What Abby needed.

No matter what, he wasn't going to run away again. Wasn't going to lose her out of fear.

He'd take a chance on fate because she had the strength to take a chance on him.

On *them*.
And he was all in.
For as long as he could have her.

Epilogue

Holiday time for the Montgomerys meant many parties, lots of drinks, and tons of food. Holiday parties, when it came to the Montgomerys in Colorado Springs, especially when that party happened to be at Thea's house, meant lots of cheese. Abby didn't understand why there was so much cheese, but she wasn't about to complain. She liked cheese, maybe not as much as Thea and Dimitri, but it was an inside joke, and she made sure to leave them as much cheese as they desired.

It had been a few days since the incident with Michael, and things were going better. So much better.

Everyone had pitched in to clean up at Teas'd, and she hadn't actually lost as much merchandise as she had feared. Insurance would take care of the rest, and because she paid a ton for insurance, they *were* going to help. Call it a holiday miracle, but the claim was actually going well.

She knocked on wood, ignoring Ryan's stare as she did. She didn't want to tempt fate, especially not during the holidays.

"What was that?"

"Just thinking."

"I don't know, you thinking can lead to dangerous things."

She elbowed him in the gut, and Ryan laughed. Julia ran up to them, and he picked her up, putting her on his hip as easily as if he'd done it a million times before. Ryan and Julia already knew each other, so introducing them wasn't that difficult. Plus, Julia was young enough that Abby didn't have to introduce him as a *special friend* where things could get awkward. But they were taking it slow. Yes, they were sleeping together. Yes, they were dating. Yes, she knew she was falling in love with him. And, yes, he was falling in love with her, but they were still new. They were going to wait until everything was just right before they took any next steps.

Because this was their relationship, their happily ever after.

Abby had a good feeling about this. She had a good feeling about a lot of things.

She was going to hire another of Thea's part-time workers for her other part-time shift. She'd had a sale right after the incident at the store and had already made her money back. Ryan and the others at Montgomery Ink Too had helped with everything, to the point where she hadn't really had to even lift a finger. She might get spoiled with that.

Her baby girl was smiling and grinning and playing with Ryan's beard.

Julia wasn't going to get confused when it came to Max or Ryan. Because Max was Daddy, and Ryan was Mommy's new friend. Maybe in the future, it would be something more, but it was okay that they were taking things slowly. It was okay that they had taken the first steps and trusted each other.

Because they'd taken long enough for this to happen, they could take as long as they wanted to get where they were going.

"Okay, time for the white elephant part of the party." Adrienne bounced to her feet, and Mace rolled his eyes.

Then he leaned forward. "Remember, there are children in the room. So this game better end PG or G. What's the one that's for their age?"

"Good to know you have this whole father thing going on." Shep rolled his eyes and brought his daughter Livvy into the living room upside down. Soon, the whole room was packed. The elder Montgomerys were sitting in an armchair, cuddling as if they were newlyweds rather than having been married for over thirty years. Mace and Adrienne were sitting on the floor, playing with Daisy as she told them about her brand-new ribbons that she had gotten already that were under the tree.

Thea and Dimitri were also cuddled on the floor, their big golden retriever, Captain, snoring lazily by the fire. The fact that he wasn't trying to rummage under the Christmas tree or tear at the wrapping paper told them just how tired the pup was. Apparently, he had gone on a hike the day before, even in the snow, and needed his old-doggie sleep.

Carter and Roxie weren't there, but then again, Carter was still healing, and the family acted as if everything were fine. Everything would be fine.

At least Abby hoped it would be.

Kaylee and Landon were in the room as well, but pointedly not sitting next to each other. Abby had a feeling they were going to figure out exactly what was going on with the pair of them soon. But finally, all Abby had eyes for was Ryan and her Julia.

"I got you something," Ryan whispered.

"Really? Which one is it? I'll try to get it from the white elephant."

He shook his head before giving her a box. "No, this one's just for you. I got something silly for the rest of them."

"No fair, you can't just hand over gifts like that," Adrienne said, her eyes dancing with laughter.

"Hey, you play your own game; this is just for Abby, thank you very much."

Abby knew her cheeks were red, but she just smiled at Ryan and took the box.

"Can I open it now?"

"Of course."

"Help?" Julia asked, and Abby nodded.

"Okay, baby girl, you help your mommy open this gift."

Abby opened her gift slowly, Julia helping with her tiny little hands while sitting on Ryan's lap. They looked such like a family, and she was really okay with that. Because they had been friends first, and that would never change.

And she was happy.

So happy.

As she looked at the new teapot Ryan had gotten her, one she knew had been made by Jake Gallagher, she just grinned up at the man she knew she was already in love with.

"I love it."

Ryan leaned forward and kissed her cheek before whispering in her year. "And I love you," he whispered.

She knew it was too soon, but she didn't care. "I love you, too."

Julia patted each of their cheeks and then kissed them both.

Ryan laughed and kissed her little girl, and then kissed her on the lips, softly.

Everybody clapped, teasing them before they went into opening up their white elephant gifts and joining in on all the other jazz that came with a Montgomery party. Abby knew that she and Ryan and Julia were on their own path, but she was falling in love with everything around her. Not just Ryan. But she loved him. And he loved her. Yes, everything had changed, but that was fine with her.

She looked over at the tree, a smaller one next to the larger one. That one only had ornaments made for Thea's friends, or ornaments that were made for everyone important in their lives.

There was one for each Montgomery, and one for each of the workers that had become part of the Montgomery family. There was one for Landon, Kaylee, Abby, Julia, and Ryan. And there were two more that brought tears to Abby's eyes when she first saw them.

One was for Michael, because there had to be hope in the darkness.

And one was for Max, because there had to be love in that hope.

And as she leaned into Ryan and blew a kiss at the ornament made for the other man that she loved, Abby knew that life might have thrown her for a loop more than once, but she always found her feet. She always found that hope, that love, and that peace.

The holidays were here, and her family was holding her close.

And she had been born once again from the ashes.

This was her life now.

New beginnings and all.

* * * *

Also from 1001 Dark Nights and Carrie Ann Ryan, discover Inked Nights, Wicked Wolf, Hidden Ink, and Adoring Ink.

Discover 1001 Dark Nights Collection Six

DRAGON CLAIMED by Donna Grant
A Dark Kings Novella

ASHES TO INK by Carrie Ann Ryan
A Montgomery Ink: Colorado Springs Novella

ENSNARED by Elisabeth Naughton
An Eternal Guardians Novella

EVERMORE by Corinne Michaels
A Salvation Series Novella

VENGEANCE by Rebecca Zanetti
A Dark Protectors/Rebels Novella

ELI'S TRIUMPH by Joanna Wylde
A Reapers MC Novella

CIPHER by Larissa Ione
A Demonica Underworld Novella

RESCUING MACIE by Susan Stoker
A Delta Force Heroes Novella

ENCHANTED by Lexi Blake
A Masters and Mercenaries Novella

TAKE THE BRIDE by Carly Phillips
A Knight Brothers Novella

INDULGE ME by J. Kenner
A Stark Ever After Novella

THE KING by Jennifer L. Armentrout
A Wicked Novella

Discover 1001 Dark Nights

COLLECTION THREE
HIDDEN INK by Carrie Ann Ryan
BLOOD ON THE BAYOU by Heather Graham
SEARCHING FOR MINE by Jennifer Probst
DANCE OF DESIRE by Christopher Rice
ROUGH RHYTHM by Tessa Bailey
DEVOTED by Lexi Blake
Z by Larissa Ione
FALLING UNDER YOU by Laurelin Paige
EASY FOR KEEPS by Kristen Proby
UNCHAINED by Elisabeth Naughton
HARD TO SERVE by Laura Kaye
DRAGON FEVER by Donna Grant
KAYDEN/SIMON by Alexandra Ivy/Laura Wright
STRUNG UP by Lorelei James
MIDNIGHT UNTAMED by Lara Adrian
TRICKED by Rebecca Zanetti
DIRTY WICKED by Shayla Black
THE ONLY ONE by Lauren Blakely
SWEET SURRENDER by Liliana Hart

COLLECTION FOUR
ROCK CHICK REAWAKENING by Kristen Ashley
ADORING INK by Carrie Ann Ryan
SWEET RIVALRY by K. Bromberg
SHADE'S LADY by Joanna Wylde
RAZR by Larissa Ione
ARRANGED by Lexi Blake
TANGLED by Rebecca Zanetti
HOLD ME by J. Kenner
SOMEHOW, SOME WAY by Jennifer Probst
TOO CLOSE TO CALL by Tessa Bailey
HUNTED by Elisabeth Naughton
EYES ON YOU by Laura Kaye
BLADE by Alexandra Ivy/Laura Wright
DRAGON BURN by Donna Grant
TRIPPED OUT by Lorelei James
STUD FINDER by Lauren Blakely

MIDNIGHT UNLEASHED by Lara Adrian
HALLOW BE THE HAUNT by Heather Graham
DIRTY FILTHY FIX by Laurelin Paige
THE BED MATE by Kendall Ryan
NIGHT GAMES by CD Reiss
NO RESERVATIONS by Kristen Proby
DAWN OF SURRENDER by Liliana Hart

COLLECTION FIVE
BLAZE ERUPTING by Rebecca Zanetti
ROUGH RIDE by Kristen Ashley
HAWKYN by Larissa Ione
RIDE DIRTY by Laura Kaye
ROME'S CHANCE by Joanna Wylde
THE MARRIAGE ARRANGEMENT by Jennifer Probst
SURRENDER by Elisabeth Naughton
INKED NIGHTS by Carrie Ann Ryan
ENVY by Rachel Van Dyken
PROTECTED by Lexi Blake
THE PRINCE by Jennifer L. Armentrout
PLEASE ME by J. Kenner
WOUND TIGHT by Lorelei James
STRONG by Kylie Scott
DRAGON NIGHT by Donna Grant
TEMPTING BROOKE by Kristen Proby
HAUNTED BE THE HOLIDAYS by Heather Graham
CONTROL by K. Bromberg
HUNKY HEARTBREAKER by Kendall Ryan
THE DARKEST CAPTIVE by Gena Showalter

Also from 1001 Dark Nights:

TAME ME by J. Kenner
THE SURRENDER GATE By Christopher Rice
SERVICING THE TARGET By Cherise Sinclair
TEMPT ME by J. Kenner

About Carrie Ann Ryan

New York Times and *USA Today* Bestselling Author Carrie Ann Ryan never thought she'd be a writer. Not really. No, she loved math and science and even went on to graduate school in chemistry. Yes, she read as a kid and devoured teen fiction and Harry Potter, but it wasn't until someone handed her a romance book in her late teens that she realized that there was something out there just for her. When another author suggested she use the voices in her head for good and not evil, The Redwood Pack and all her other stories were born.

Carrie Ann is a bestselling author of over twenty novels and novellas and has so much more on her mind (and on her spreadsheets *grins*) that she isn't planning on giving up her dream anytime soon.

www.CarrieAnnRyan.com

Discover More Carrie Ann Ryan

Inked Nights: A Montgomery Ink Novella
By Carrie Ann Ryan

Tattoo artist, Derek Hawkins knows the rules:
  One night a month.
  No last names.
  No promises.

Olivia Madison has her own rules:
  Don't fall in love.
  No commitment.
  Never tell Derek the truth.

When their worlds crash into each other however, Derek and Olivia will have to face what they fought to ignore as well as the connection they tried to forget.

* * * *

Adoring Ink: A Montgomery Ink Novella
By Carrie Ann Ryan

Holly Rose fell in love with a Montgomery, but left him when he couldn't love her back. She might have been the one to break the ties and ensure her ex's happy ending, but now Holly's afraid she's missed out on more than a chance at forever. Though she's always been the dependable good girl, she's ready to take a leap of faith and embark on the journey of a lifetime.

Brody Deacon loves ink, women, fast cars, and living life like there's no tomorrow. The thing is, he doesn't know if he *has* a tomorrow at all. When he sees Holly, he's not only intrigued, he also hears the warnings of danger in his head. She's too sweet, too innocent, and way too special for him. But when Holly asks him to help her grab the bull by the horns, he can't help but go all in.

As they explore Holly's bucket list and their own desires, Brody will have to make sure he doesn't fall too hard and too fast. Sometimes, people think happily ever afters don't happen for everyone, and Brody will have to face his demons and tell Holly the truth of what it means to truly live life to the fullest…even when they're both running out of time.

* * * *

Hidden Ink: A Montgomery Ink Novella
By Carrie Ann Ryan

The Montgomery Ink series continues with the long-awaited romance between the café owner next door and the tattoo artist who's loved her from afar.

Hailey Monroe knows the world isn't always fair, but she's picked herself up from the ashes once before and if she needs to, she'll do it again. It's been years since she first spotted the tattoo artist with a scowl that made her heart skip a beat, but now she's finally gained the courage to approach him. Only it won't be about what their future could bring, but how to finish healing the scars from her past.

Sloane Gordon lived through the worst kinds of hell yet the temptation next door sends him to another level. He's kept his distance because he knows what kind of man he is versus what kind of man Hailey needs. When she comes to him with a proposition that sends his mind whirling and his soul shattering, he'll do everything in his power to protect the woman he cares for and the secrets he's been forced to keep.

* * * *

Wicked Wolf: A Redwood Pack Novella
By Carrie Ann Ryan

The war between the Redwood Pack and the Centrals is one of wolf legend. Gina Eaton lost both of her parents when a member of their

Pack betrayed them. Adopted by the Alpha of the Pack as a child, Gina grew up within the royal family to become an enforcer and protector of her den. She's always known fate can be a tricky and deceitful entity, but when she finds the one man that could be her mate, she might throw caution to the wind and follow the path set out for her, rather than forging one of her own.

Quinn Weston's mate walked out on him five years ago, severing their bond in the most brutal fashion. She not only left him a shattered shadow of himself, but their newborn son as well. Now, as the lieutenant of the Talon Pack's Alpha, he puts his whole being into two things: the safety of his Pack and his son.

When the two Alphas put Gina and Quinn together to find a way to ensure their treaties remain strong, fate has a plan of its own. Neither knows what will come of the Pack's alliance, let alone one between the two of them. The past paved their paths in blood and heartache, but it will take the strength of a promise and iron will to find their future.

Hidden Ink

A Montgomery Ink Novella
By Carrie Ann Ryan

The Montgomery Ink series continues with the long-awaited romance between the café owner next door and the tattoo artist who's loved her from afar.

Hailey Monroe knows the world isn't always fair, but she's picked herself up from the ashes once before and if she needs to, she'll do it again. It's been years since she first spotted the tattoo artist with a scowl that made her heart skip a beat, but now she's finally gained the courage to approach him. Only it won't be about what their future could bring, but how to finish healing the scars from her past.

Sloane Gordon lived through the worst kinds of hell yet the temptation next door sends him to another level. He's kept his distance because he knows what kind of man he is versus what kind of man Hailey needs. When she comes to him with a proposition that sends his mind whirling and his soul shattering, he'll do everything in his power to protect the woman he cares for and the secrets he's been forced to keep.

* * * *

Hailey was still a blank canvas, but knew she eventually wanted ink of her own.

One day she would be brave enough to ask for it.

It wasn't the ink she was afraid of, wasn't the needles. God knew she'd seen enough of those in her life thanks to chemo, radiation, and the countless tests and treatments.

No, it was the person she wanted to do her ink.

While Maya, Austin, and Callie would bend over backward to help her with her tattoo and the nerves that came with it, she didn't want them to do it. She had someone else in mind.

Someone she was afraid to talk to for fear of what would spill out.

Someone who didn't care for her as she cared for him.

Hailey's phone buzzed and she sighed. Today was a day for melancholy thoughts, apparently. She turned off the timer on her phone then went to the front of the café to flip the sign to *Open* while unlocking the door. Two of her morning regulars, men in business suits, who had the courtesy to get off their phones before they walked into the shop, smiled at her.

"Good morning, gentlemen," she said with a smile. "Your usuals?"

"You know it," one said.

"Of course," the other one added in.

She smiled widely then went back to her counter to get their drinks and pastries. Soon her help would be there to work the register so she wouldn't be alone. The crisp morning air had filtered in with the brief opening and closing of the door, and as she worked quickly, she knew today would be a good day.

Any day she could do what she loved would be a better day than the last.

By the time Corrine came in and took over the front station, Hailey was already buzzing with the adrenaline of a morning rush. There was nothing like earning a living doing something she loved. The brownies were a hit, and the first batch she'd set out was soon gone. Normally, she would have saved them for the afternoon crowd so customers would eat her bagels and other morning delights, but she didn't have the heart to hide them in the back. Nor did she have the will.

She'd have eaten the whole batch and gained all that weight Callie had joked about. Lying on the kitchen floor in a sugar coma wasn't the best way to run a bakery.

The morning passed by quickly, and soon, Hailey found herself in a slight lull. After talking to Corrine, she made a tray of pastries and to-go cups of coffee—each one individualized for someone special. She wasn't sure exactly who was working today over at Montgomery Ink, but she knew at least the main people would be there, and she was familiar with their drink of choice. Even if she made extra, nothing would go to waste. Austin and Maya would make sure of that.

Hailey made her way through the door and held back a sigh at the sound of needles buzzing and the deep voices of those speaking. She loved Montgomery Ink. It was part of her home.

"Caffeine! I want to have your babies. Can I have your babies, sexy momma?" Maya asked as she cradled her coffee and cheese pastry.

Hailey snorted. "Are you talking to me or the coffee?"

Maya blinked up at her, the ring in her brow glittering under the lights. "Yes."

Hailey just shook her head and handed off a drink to Austin, who bussed a kiss on her cheek. His beard tickled her, and once again, she wanted to bow down at Sierra's feet in jealousy. Seriously, the man was hot. All the Montgomerys were.

Soon she found herself with only one drink on her tray along with a single cherry and cream cheese pastry.

His favorite.

Behind Maya's work area sat another station.

Sloane Gordon's.

All six-foot-four, two hundred something pounds of muscle covered in ink, his light brown skin accented perfectly by the designs. The man was sex. All sex. Sloane had shaved his head years ago. She was convinced he kept it shaved just to turn her on. He kept his beard trimmed, but that and the bald head apparently jump-started a new kink in her.

Who knew?

He was a decade older than Hailey, and though he didn't speak of it, she knew he'd been through war, battle, and heartbreak.

And she loved him.

Only he didn't *see* her. He never took a step toward her. He also looked as if he were ready to growl at her presence most of the time.

Much like he did now.

On behalf of 1001 Dark Nights,
Liz Berry and M.J. Rose would like to thank ~

Steve Berry
Doug Scofield
Kim Guidroz
Jillian Stein
InkSlinger PR
Dan Slater
Asha Hossain
Chris Graham
Fedora Chen
Kasi Alexander
Jessica Johns
Dylan Stockton
Richard Blake
and Simon Lipskar

Made in the USA
Columbia, SC
14 January 2019